Courting

Intrigue

WENDY MAY ANDREWS

☙ℰ☙

Sparrow Ink
www.sparrowdeck.com

ISBN - 978-1-989634-08-0

www.wendymayandrews.com

Security or loyalty? Attraction or duty?
How does one choose?

Miss Lillian Shaw, wellborn but impoverished, has been living with her aunt, the widowed Viscountess Shepley, since the death of her parents a few years ago. Lily wants to find a paid position to add to her savings so she can open a bakery when she receives the Byram Bequest. Her aunt would rather present her and arrange a High Society marriage for her. Lily's limited experience with the gentry has not been positive, and she would prefer to be independent than tied for life to a noble lout.

The Earl of Sedgwick only wants to go home and see to his estates after his sudden, unexpected inheritance but has one last investigation to complete for the Home Office. When his path crosses that of Miss Shaw, he is intrigued by the attractive young woman but forces himself to keep his focus on the matter at hand.

When Lily becomes suspicious of the earl's activities, he must decide whether or not to bring her into his confidence. Lily is forced to choose between her security and her loyalties while Sedgwick is torn between his attraction and his duty.

Dedication

In this book everyone is trying to be so brave and independent while they really need to team up and conquer their circumstances. I think this is a common occurrence. We all want to be fierce and independent when we really need a friend or partner. So this book is for everyone looking for their teammates, friends, family of the heart. You'll get there.

Acknowledgements

My books wouldn't happen without the support of my fabulous hubby. He helps in so many ways — listening to the stories as they unfold, keeping track of my characters, formatting my manuscripts, ordering dinner when I've been too caught up in the story to cook. I'm blessed to have my own real-life hero.

My parents are my biggest fans, supporting and cheering for me every step of the way. I wouldn't have life without them, nor would I enjoy it nearly as much.

My beta readers — Marlene, Suzanne, Monique, Alfred, and Christina — help me immeasurably. Their help with the story as well as care and compassion for the author are a blessing.

Les at GermanCreative keeps making me better and better covers. Thank you so much!

Julie Sherwood's edits are amazing. Any remaining errors are the author's.

Chapter One

L ily was standing at the window, gazing across the vast grounds at Ashburn Place, when she saw the group of men emerging from the copse of trees. *They must have been hunting*, she thought with an absent shudder, a sport she loathed. She understood killing meat for food, of course, but why would they hunt something just for the fun of killing it? How could that even be considered *fun?*

She would have stepped back from the window for fear of her aunt's stepson seeing her if not for the fact that her attention was ensnared by the bright blue gaze of the most arresting man she had ever seen. He wasn't classically handsome, but his high cheekbones and direct, intelligent scrutiny were attractive in a way she had never experienced before. His chestnut coloured hair was windblown. She could tell it was thick, even from this distance, and her hand twitched with an instinctive desire to reach out and run her fingers through it.

Feeling a frown forming on her face, Lily tried to break from the trance-like experience, but she felt as though her eyes were locked with his. It made no sense. If he was a friend of Lester, he should automatically be of no interest to her. She should be repulsed. So, why was she so enthralled? She finally realized her aunt was talking to her, and she managed to tear her gaze away.

"Oh, my dear, I just feel dreadful about the awkward situation my stepson is putting us in."

"Aunt Vi, please, I beg of you, do not let it trouble you. I certainly shan't."

"But I so wanted him to provide you with a dowry so that you could have a Season and you could marry some lovely, handsome, rich lord and live happily ever after."

Lily had to grin. Her aunt was the only living relative she had, but she was such an idealistic romantic. "Darling Vi, you know that wasn't to be my destiny. If you hadn't married Uncle Wilbur, there wouldn't have even been the slightest possibility of a Season for me. You and my father grew up in genteel poverty, as did my mother. As did I. It was only when Uncle Wilbur took such a shine to you that all of our situations improved."

"And if he hadn't gone and died on me, he would have been sure to provide you with a dowry and a Season and would have enjoyed every second of it."

Offering her aunt a fond smile, Lillian knew the words were the truth. Uncle Wilbur had the softest heart and would have done anything to bring a smile to his wife's face. Theirs was a love match. A late marriage for both of them. Wilbur's first wife had died along with their younger son. The widower had taken a long time to overcome the dual loss and hadn't any desire to have more babies. So, he was in a position to be able to marry for love, find a comfortable partner for his old age, and under no obligation to seek a young wife to provide him with children. Aunt Vi would have been a lovely mother, but it hadn't worked out that way for her. So, she did her very best to mother Lillian whenever she had the opportunity.

"You know you're the daughter neither of us had the opportunity to have."

"I know."

"He should have made it official in his Will."

"Aunt Vi, don't let yourself get into a taking. You know Uncle Wilbur was still a vital, strong man when he died. He had absolutely no intention of leaving us. He should still be here now. But that's not the way it worked out. And we have to accept that rather than rail against it. And really, it's not so very bad. Having gotten to know your stepson over time, I'm not so sure I would have wanted to marry into the aristocracy anyway."

"They aren't all like him, I can assure you."

"Since I've only known two noblemen, one was lovely, one not so much, it doesn't inspire me with confidence. One out of two isn't a good ratio."

Violet grinned. "There you go with your maths again. That wouldn't have done at a London ball, that's for sure."

"All the more reason to be glad I'm not going to be attending, then, isn't it?"

"Oh, but what about your future? What is to become of you once I've passed on?"

"Violet Anne Shaw Shepley, do not speak to me of your death. We have had far too much loss in the past two years. I will not contemplate the possibility of any other. If Lester will not allow me to remain here as your companion, I will find a position elsewhere. I can be either a governess or a lady's companion. It's only for a few more years, anyway. I will receive the Byram Bequest when I turn twenty-five, even if I haven't found a mate. Then I will open my bakery. It will be quite lovely."

"But do you truly want to go into trade, my dear?"

Lily grinned. "Your few years as a Lady have coloured your judgment, Aunt Vi. My father was in trade despite being the descendant of a younger son of a younger son of some noble. We did just fine. Genteel poverty is not enjoyable. I will never be cold or hungry again if I have a bakery."

"Oh dear, oh dear, but it will eliminate all prospects for you. I truly thought we had decided the bakery wasn't for you."

"You had decided that, Aunt Vi. I still think it is the perfect idea. I even know exactly where I will have it. I will go back to Sherton and start there. While the countess has her kitchen staff already, I know she occasionally hires out some of the baking for larger events. I will be in the right place at the right time for once in my life."

"But don't you want to marry someday? You're still quite young."

"Nearly on the shelf at almost twenty-one, am I not? No one has wanted me in my strange in-between circumstances. Not quite aristocracy, not quite bourgeois, not quite a servant. It's complicated. I don't want a pity marriage or a marriage of a different type of servitude. I want a love match like you or Mama had, or nothing at all. And I don't really see that happening for me amongst your precious nobles."

Lily regretted her plain speaking when her volatile aunt started dabbing at the corners of her eyes with a handkerchief, but then she caught the edge of the smile her devious aunt was trying to hide.

"You sneak! You're trying to make me feel badly about what I said, and yet you agree with me."

Violet tried to protest. "I don't agree with you! I just don't disagree with you. I would rather you were married to a rich man, or at least one who was comfortably situated so you wouldn't have to work so hard. Opening a bakery sounds terribly difficult. And do you really think ten pounds will be enough to get you off the ground?"

"I do really think it will. But I can't have the ten pounds until I hit the ripe old age of twenty-five and am a spinster."

"You really think you would prefer it?" Aunt Vi's dubious tone made Lily's naturally good humour return.

"I really do. I know you and Uncle Wilbur were happy, but I have never met a man who made me even consider taking that chance."

"But you've barely met anyone. Maybe one of Lester's friends could prove to be suitable."

Lily knew the withering look she cast at her aunt wasn't in the least respectful, but there was no way she would consider anyone who would have Lester as his friend.

"Aunt Violet, surely you wouldn't seriously offer me such a suggestion."

"No, I suppose you're right. He is rather dreadful, isn't he?"

Lily smiled. Her aunt's perpetually sunny humour made her see the best in everyone, even Lester most of the time, so if even she realized he was dreadful, it was a testament to how truly awful the man was.

A shiver slithered down Lily's back as she remembered the first time she had met the man. She had just turned fourteen and was visiting her aunt and uncle for the first time. Lester had been sent down from university for some infraction, although she had never heard the details of the story. Insolent and overly filled with his own importance, Lester thought he was entitled to everything in his sight. Including Lily. He hadn't expected her to know how to defend herself. Nor had he expected his father to banish him from the house for the duration of Lily's month-long visit. It had not been an auspicious beginning to their familial relationship. He had resented her ever since.

When Lord Wilbur died, Lester had tried to banish Aunt Violet, but the Will had been clear. Ashburn Place was not entailed. There was no Dower House to send her to. Aunt Vi was entitled to live out her days there, even if Lester were to marry. Of course, if he did marry, that could make things uncomfortable for Lady Violet, but Lily doubted any woman would be crazy enough to accept Lester, even if he were in a hurry to marry.

There were other estates, but this was the nicest one, from what Lily had been able to tell. Not that she had visited all of her uncle's holdings, but she knew Lord Wilbur had preferred spending most of his time at Ashburn Place, only visiting his other properties on occasion, in order to check on them. It would seem Lester was following in his father's footsteps now that he had inherited. Not that he was likely to actually check on the other properties. He was a lazy lout and was leaving the care of everything to his steward and Lady Violet. Which meant it was actually falling to Lillian. Which made it all the more ridiculous that he wanted her gone.

He didn't actually have the power to send her packing, but he could make her life miserable. Lillian was torn as to what to do. Her aunt wanted her to stay, but Lillian knew Lester's treatment caused Violet distress. On the other hand, Lillian was afraid of what Lester might do to her aunt if she wasn't there to protect the older woman. It wasn't as though she thought the bounder would resort to violence against her, but Lillian knew he could be exceedingly disagreeable.

A case in point was this hunting party. Lester had been up to London for some weeks, only having returned two days ago accompanied by a group of young men. Of course, it was his property so Lily didn't begrudge him his friends. But they were wild men, who couldn't be trusted. She and Violet had been dining in their rooms since the party had arrived. Now Lester had informed Vi he wanted to host a proper house party, and she needed to be the hostess.

This news had sent Violet into a fret. She had never hosted such an entertainment before and was panicking as to how to go about it. Lillian was hard pressed to soothe her.

"Have you not attended a house party before, Vi? I was certain you had told me about them on occasion. Mama and I had enjoyed imagining what it might be like."

"Well, yes, I've been to house parties before."

"And did you host dinner parties for Uncle Wilbur?"

"Oh, yes, of course, on many occasions."

"So then, it won't be so very bad, will it?"

"Well, no, I suppose not. It's just that I don't actually want to be with Lester and his friends. And you have said you won't attend. It will be dreadful."

Lillian grinned. "I'll make sure everything is at the ready for you, have no fear. You know very well that Lester would fly into a temper if I was to attend, so it's not really that I'm refusing. And you love every single person you encounter, so I really doubt you'll find it so very dreadful. From the looks of the guest list, it won't even be vulgar. It seems an invitation to Ashburn Place still holds sway, even if Lester is the current owner."

Lily's words had the desired effect. Lady Violet smiled and nodded, seeming to grow eager for the upcoming event. Lily sighed and pulled some paper from her aunt's desk.

"Shall we begin planning the meals? I'll have to speak with the housekeeper and Cook if we're to ensure all the ingredients are fully stocked."

"Oh, this is going to be such fun! Do you think we ought to plan a ball for the end? Surely you could attend that. Lester might not even notice you. We could invite the gentry from all the surrounding estates. It could be quite lovely. We have such a magnificent ballroom, it seems rather a shame that it never gets used."

Lily couldn't decide if she was dismayed or thrilled with the idea, but she couldn't deny that it was a sound thought for the house party. She just wasn't sure if she ought to attend. She dismissed the thought for the present time. It could wait for later. The additional guests would be arriving within the next couple of days, so that needed to take uppermost position in her mind for now.

Chapter Two

B rock had never been so preoccupied with a woman's face before. He hadn't been able to tear his eyes away from her and then was disappointed to the depths of his toes when she disappeared from view. Now, he couldn't get her from his mind. It was ridiculous, since she must be one of the chambermaids, and he never dallied with the servants. He was of the opinion that their lives were difficult enough without putting them in such an awkward position. He knew this put him in the minority amongst the aristocracy, but he didn't much care for the other men's opinions. But this particular young woman intrigued him. He had seen intelligence and judgment in her gaze. He could tell she didn't much care for the hunting party. That had been abundantly clear from the expressive twist of her face. Not that he could blame her. He didn't want to be there either, but it was a necessary evil. He was investigating Lester and had befriended him as part of his efforts.

Befriended was not the right word. Brock would never consider someone like Lester to be a friend. The young man was loathsome. But as the Earl of Sedgwick, Brock was a Peer, and the two had encountered one another occasionally. As soon as Brock had hinted that he would be interested in the hunting at Ashburn Place, a party had been organized. Now, the reprobate was going to add ladies to the party because one of the other young men had mentioned the desire. Brock shook his head. Lester had too much money and too little brains. He wondered if the estate would be able to bear up. Wilbur had been a good custodian of his estates and had surely left them in fine form for his heir. Brock shook his head in wonder how the heir could have fallen so far from the original.

For a split second, he actually thought about asking Lester who the woman was but then pushed the thought from his mind. He didn't want to draw attention to such beauty. The other men would not be so restrained as Brock. He wouldn't trust them with his enemy's daughter, let alone whomever that lovely creature had been.

With a sigh, Brock tried to dismiss all thought of the woman. She would only be a distraction he couldn't afford. He dragged his attention back to whatever pap Lester was spouting now.

"Since Henry was adamant that ladies were needed, and he convinced me that he had not meant ladies of the night, my stepmother has dispatched the invitations, and we'll be having a proper house party here in a matter of days."

Brock stifled his groan. Just what he needed, even more people to dilute his opportunities to pry into Lester's nefarious affairs. Or perhaps it WAS just what he needed. More people would make his movements far less obvious. If the party was larger, he couldn't be expected to be in company with Lester at all times. These arriving ladies would need escorts, of course. They could also get in his way and make his search more difficult, but really, what was he going to do? Tell the man to refuse his invited guests? That wouldn't draw unnecessary attention now would it, Brock? He couldn't help grinning as he heard the sarcasm dripping from even his thoughts. He needed this task to be over with. It was twisting him too much.

"How long did you say they were staying? I need to see to my own estates one of these days."

The others made jeering noises, ribbing him for his responsibilities. Brock took it in stride, grinning good naturedly.

"Lester knows now. Since he's inherited, he is well aware he can't be as carefree as he once was."

Lester shrugged. "Sure I can, that's what stewards are for. I let the stepmother look after that along with her wretched niece. Can't get rid of them, they might as well make themselves useful."

Brock's eyes strayed back to the window. Interesting. Perhaps that was who he had seen. He hadn't realized Wilbur's widow had remained in residence. He couldn't blame her for absenting herself while Lester was entertaining. Brock wondered if he would meet the stepmother and her niece during the house party.

She doesn't matter, Brock reminded himself. *You have a mission that needs finishing so you can return to your own estate and see to matters. The Home Office promised if you got this last one done they'd set you free. Stay focused.*

The others were tramping toward the house and Brock hurried to catch up with them. He was older than most of them by at least five years, but it felt like decades as he listened to their chatter. They reminded him of schoolboys sent down from Eton for the first time. He felt like a grandfather. He had seen too much. All he wanted to do now was curl up in front of a fire at his home and pour over the ledgers. If that made him crazy, he didn't very much care.

The worst thing about this particular mission was that he didn't actually think Lester meant to be a traitor. Brock figured he was just a dissipated, bored aristocrat that got into his cups and made some bad decisions. Lester might not even realize what he had done. But all the more reason Brock needed to get his hands on the evidence of what else was going on, so the bigger picture could be sorted out. Lester was a Peer. Brock rather thought the Home Office wasn't going to want to prosecute him if it could be proven he wasn't involved in the planning or executing of the treachery. Brock figured it would be easy enough to prove. The man was too stupid and lazy to have had any part in the background of the attack. They just needed to find out what else was going on. Then Lester could carry on his merry way down to the bottom of the brandy bottle.

Why the young men all thought it was a delightful activity to drink themselves under the table each night, Brock couldn't fathom. He hated the ache in his head and the fuzz in his mouth the morning after such benders, so he had learned young not to overindulge. Being with these youngsters and watching them get wasted was one of the worst parts of this assignment. But it was almost the most useful time. If he could feign drunkenness, which wasn't difficult at all when everyone else really was, he could ask all sorts of questions they wouldn't even remember answering the next day.

So, he had two nights before the house party expanded to ask whatever he wanted. Then he would begin his search of the property. He was lucky that he had been able to find out that Lester never visited his other properties. It would have been far more difficult to trump up an excuse to go there. Getting invited to Ashburn Place for a bit of hunting was an easy thing to accomplish. Getting the oaf to travel any further would have been a trial. But Brock would have done it. He wanted out, and this was his way. He would get what he needed and retire to the country. Nothing sounded sweeter. He would happily raise a glass with these young, entitled, loafers every night of the week if it meant he was that much closer to the quiet life he craved. And if the spot next to him was empty in front of the fire, Brock decided he didn't care. He could get cats, he thought with a grin. Besides, he wasn't even thirty. He could sit by his fire and rest for a few years before he needed to concern himself overly with the succession.

Of course, he knew it was something to consider. He, himself, was never supposed to inherit, so he was well aware of the fact that things happen. But there were some long lost cousins somewhere in the family tree who could take over if worse came to worst. Brock refused to be rushed into matrimony. He wanted his rest before he took up any more responsibilities. The thought of filling his nursery made him shudder. He'd had enough lives in his hands on the Peninsula. He didn't want to be in charge of babies any time soon, maybe not ever. Of course, that was the way of the succession, he reminded himself. His thoughts were starting to annoy him, so he was happy to accept the glass Lester handed him and tossed it back eagerly. He could happily take a little bit of oblivion right about now.

A while later, as though he couldn't help himself, Brock finally asked the question that was burning in the back of his mind. "Why do you say the niece is wretched?"

"What?" Lester was already dazed from the drink.

"You said you can't get rid of your stepmother and her wretched niece. Why do you say she's wretched? Is she ugly or merely a shrew?"

Lester tossed back the rest of his glass and muttered under his breath before clearing his throat and answering. "Both, I'd say. My father's wife puts up such a fuss that I can't rid my house of her, but I've told her if she gets out of line at all, I'll disregard them both and the mealy mouthed niece can find herself someone else to sponge off of."

Brock knew he ought to keep himself well out of it but every fiber in his gentleman's soul was crying out to say something to the lout. He grunted, allowing it to sound rather drunken. "It's always the same, isn't it? It's the lot of those who inherit to look after all the hangers-on. Like you could never throw out your old nanny, right?"

Despite how addled he was from the liquor, Lester looked at him as though he had lost his mind. "You're jesting, right? I certainly can't be bothered with the servants. If they aren't of any use to me anymore, I don't need 'em around."

Brock couldn't respond, but there was a low murmur of dissent from the young noblemen. Despite their dissipation and their misguided friendship with the viscount, most of the young men had been raised from the cradle with a certain sense of what was owed to others and a strong duty to being a gentleman. They might be playing at the life of a rake, but they knew there was a certain line.

Lester must have realized he was treading on dangerous ground. He looked around the group, gave an awkward chuckle and held up the decanter.

"Are we going to chatter like old women or are we going to satisfy our thirst?"

His friends laughed and cheered, holding up their glasses, and Brock fought not to roll his eyes. He needed to finish his mission. Fast.

Chapter Three

T he early morning air was turning Lily's cheeks pink and trying to pull her hair from its pins as she made her way back to the house. She had needed the fresh air. Lillian was starting to feel like a prisoner in the large house. Trying to avoid Lester's guests while still making all the arrangements for the house party was a full-time occupation, made all the more complicated by not attending or meeting any of the visitors.

Lillian didn't mind, for the most part, but the desire to leave the house had required an extra early rising that day. And she hated getting up extra early. But in the end, it had been worth it. The sunrise had been spectacular and well worth the effort required to see it. It was just what she needed to clear the cobwebs from her mind and the fidgets from her body. The long walk to the cliff had been the perfect escape when she decided she couldn't take another day cooped up in the large house.

"Good morning."

Lillian nearly shrieked but managed to cut the sound off so only a low gurgle came out. She had been so caught up in her own thoughts that she hadn't noticed the tall man standing inside the copse of trees. She put her hand over her mouth, lowered her head, and would have marched right by him without even acknowledging his greeting, if he hadn't put his hand out to stop her.

"Do they not teach manners around here?" His inquiry sent hot colour flooding her cheeks.

"Certainly they do, but we have not been introduced, so we cannot converse." Her reply sounded haughty, but she didn't care as she raised her chin and stared down her nose at him. She had seen Wilbur do that on occasion to good effect and hadn't even realized she was capable of the action.

It didn't have the desired effect. The handsome man grinned.

"We're in the country, not at some *ton* event. Surely there would be no harm in acknowledging someone's greeting."

Lillian shrugged. "I'm actually in rather a hurry and don't have time for idle chit chat."

The man's eyes scoured her face and all of her, making Lillian squirm inside. She had thrown on the most comfortable old gown she owned for the hike to the cliff. It wasn't as though she owned anything of high fashion, but the handsome man made her wish she had at least given a modicum of thought to her appearance before she had left her chamber.

"Something tells me you wouldn't know how to engage in anything so idle as chit chat, even if you had the time. You're the niece aren't you?"

"I beg your pardon?" she replied, flummoxed by both his observation and his question. The man had assessed her and identified her in one sweep of his curious gaze. A reluctant sense of familiarity shimmied through her.

"I saw you in the window almost a week ago. Why have you not joined the guests?"

"Is that really any of your affair?" She wasn't about to explain her complicated circumstances to this handsome nobleman. Lillian felt the heat flooding her cheeks, and she raised her chin higher to counteract it, not wanting this stranger to think she was ashamed. She couldn't fathom why she was blushing. It was most annoying.

He grinned in response to her question. "Not really, but I admit to unending curiosity. Unless you have put yourself beyond the pale in some way, I cannot imagine any circumstance in which the countess' niece is not welcome in polite society."

"Of course not." Lillian didn't elaborate. Wrenching her arm from his grasp, she allowed her long strides to take her away from the tempting presence of the handsome man. *Why would my mind even supply the word* tempting *in its description,* she wondered before answering herself. She was tempted to stay and visit with the handsome man, enjoying his intelligent gaze. *I am just as foolish as the other women,* she thought with disgust.

She had, for the most part, been able to flit through the house unobtrusively, even when the guests were present, ensuring that everything was in order for the party. She had observed the young ladies giggling over the handsome friends Lester had brought down from London with him. Lillian had thought them insipid. But here she was, wanting to fawn over the beautiful man just because he had condescended to speak with her. She could just imagine what he wanted to talk about. She had put Lester in his place when she was fourteen when he tried to have just such a conversation. She wasn't about to put up with it from a stranger, no matter how delicious he looked.

Lillian felt the man's gaze boring between her shoulder blades as she stalked back to the house, but she didn't turn back to look at him. She was relieved that he also didn't chase after her. From the size of him, she wouldn't have been able to outrun him or fight him off if he had been of a mind to exert his power over her. She was furious with herself. She shouldn't have been out alone with Lester and his friends in residence. But she had thought they would all be abed until noon at least. Thus was Lester's pattern whenever he was in residence, and she didn't see his friends being any different while they were there. But it had been foolish of her and would not be repeated. She would just have to reconcile herself to the imprisonment until Lester left again.

Really, it wasn't so bad, she reminded herself. It was a large house. Even calling it a house was a rather ridiculous misuse of the word. It was bordering on palatial, but since Lester was only a viscount, it couldn't really be called that. Nonetheless, Ashburn Place was huge. Uncle Wilbur's ancestors must have had large families and many retainers. Then of course, too, one had to always be prepared to entertain the monarch, so there was a section of the Place that was particularly spectacular. Lillian loved to dust that room. It was not at all an occupation for a gently bred female, but she didn't care. There was so little that was conventional about her, why shouldn't she enjoy dusting? It didn't hurt anybody. And it gave her an excuse to be in that part of the house.

Lester wouldn't really care, as long as she stayed out of his way, where she was. And as long as she stayed out of sight of his guests, of course. Lillian realized she should have told the strange man not to mention her to Lester. Hopefully he wouldn't have any realization of who she was, she thought until she remembered he did know who she was. He had called her "the niece." Someone must have mentioned her. Lillian's stomach clenched, and her heart sank.

Had Aunt Violet been matchmaking? Didn't she realize that Lester would make both their lives miserable if he thought Lillian was stepping out of line? Maybe she really should look for a position. She had enough experience she could probably even get a position as housekeeper, but without a reference no one would hire her. Aunt Violet would provide her a reference for a position as a governess or companion, but Lillian was afraid those might bore her, considering all that she had been able to take on here at Ashburn. But getting away from here would be safer.

All she had to do was keep herself safe for four more years. Four years. At the moment, that felt like an eternity. But her parents had already been gone for more than three years, and it was hard to believe that the time had disappeared so quickly. Surely, the four years would be here and gone without too much trouble.

Lillian sighed. There could be lots of trouble if she wasn't a little more careful. And she did love being here with Aunt Violet. She sighed again. If only Wilbur's Will had been written a little more carefully.

Casting the melancholy thoughts from her mind, Lillian reached her room and quickly changed into her gown that most resembled the maid's uniforms. It was the best for blending in. She was able to arrange everything for the house party without anyone realizing she was even there. She had noticed years ago that the nobility almost never noticed the servants unless something was going wrong. Lillian ensured nothing went wrong. It kept her from their notice. It was an ideal situation for her peace of mind.

She loved the large building and all its occupants. All, that was, except Lester, of course. If only Uncle *Wilbur hadn't died so suddenly*, she thought and felt her chin wobble. Shoving that thought away, Lillian slipped into the housekeeper's small office.

"Good morning, dearie," the pleasant older woman greeted.

Lillian hugged the comfortable older woman. "Good morning, Mrs. Parker. How is your leg feeling today?"

"Much improved, thanks to that ointment you gave me, thank you, dearie. How are things coming along with Master Lester's friends?"

"It's quite smooth. You'd hardly believe they were here. Those new maids you hired are working out very well."

Mrs. Parker giggled. "Get on with you, dearie. I hired. As if. You know I only did what you suggested."

Lillian grinned. "Well, then we make an excellent team, don't we?"

"I would certainly say so, especially with my leg acting up. I wouldn't be able to keep up with everything if you weren't here to help out your aunt like you do."

"Aunt Violet appreciates everything you are still able to do, Mrs. P. And you'll be back on your feet before you know it, I'm sure."

"I hope so, dearie, but I'm afraid that it won't be before his lordship is back to Town and all his guests with him."

"Well, hopefully they'll all be moving along before too awfully long, so we needn't worry about it."

"It's a lot for you to take on though, dearie. It isn't quite right."

"Now Mrs. P, don't tell me you're going to try to curtail my fun."

They exchanged conspiratorial smiles, and the older woman leaned back on her cushions. "That would be mighty foolish of me, now wouldn't it?"

Lillian laughed and left the room. "I'll be down in the kitchens for a bit. Ring if you need anything."

The older woman frowned. "That certainly wouldn't be right."

Lillian hated it when the servants got starchy with her. It couldn't be helped, though, when they remembered that she was actually gentry. It didn't happen very often, but every once in a while they realized she wasn't actually one of them. It would have been funny if it weren't so very awkward. She didn't bother acknowledging the housekeeper's words.

Venturing into the kitchens was a highlight of Lily's day. The warm scents usually combined so pleasantly. She actually gave thought to that when she was planning the menus. It was dreadful when fish was being cooked. She very rarely planned a menu with fish. Certainly not when any baking was to be done.

Lily wished she could find a position as a housekeeper in some large estate. But the only way to get hired as a housekeeper was to have stellar references, and no one was going to give her any references for what she was doing here at Ashburn Place. No one in a position to provide references would be willing to admit what she had been doing here. Lily stifled another sigh. But she could find a position as lady's companion, and she might be able to do the same thing. It would just be more awkward. And fraught with the potential for more problems. It was hard to imagine facing more problems than she faced here, but Aunt Violet didn't give her any resistance for what she wanted to do around the place. Another Lady might. And Aunt Violet had been right when she said an older woman needing to hire a companion was probably not the sweetest lady to spend time with or she would have a friend or family member to do it rather than needing to hire someone.

But Lily couldn't stay in this limbo for much longer. With Lester hating her and banishing her from being seen, it made an uncomfortable situation for everyone. It made it impossible to actually BE Aunt Violet's companion. And it wasn't as though Lily *wanted* to stay here. She loved the Place and her aunt, but she needed to get away from Lester. Starting a fresh life somewhere else would help her overcome her grief, too, she hoped. It had already been three years since she'd lost her parents. One year since Wilbur had died. Aunt Violet was finally out of her blacks and back into her favourite colour. It was wonderful that shades of purple were allowed even in half mourning. Lily couldn't wait to see her in the gown they had selected for the ball at the end of the house party. It was the perfect shade to complement her name, a vibrant violet. She would look lovely.

Lillian was almost certain her aunt wouldn't consider remarriage, but there would certainly be some gentlemen vying for her hand for the dance floor at the very least. It would be lovely. Lily felt a pang and realized it was envy, but she shoved the thought away. How could she be envious of a woman's widowhood? She just wished she would be allowed to dance, is all. She never had done so in a real ballroom at an actual ball. Just practicing with her parents in their old house in the tiny little parlour where they spent all their time.

Allowing her mind to wander back there wasn't really a luxury she had time for, but she allowed it for a moment, as a source of comfort. The room had really been sad and shabby, Lily realized now due to the constant comparison with the luxury of Ashburn Place, but none of its occupants had cared. That room had always been full of laughter and love. The fraying furnishings had not mattered one jot.

The walls were lined with their favourite books. The view from the windows had been tranquil and charming. And they could fill that room with laughter or music and dancing every night of the week, if they had so chosen. Lily's parents had been well loved by everyone around them. Friends would visit frequently. Their door was never barred against anyone needing help, even though they were never plump in the pocket themselves. But they had never gone hungry. Lily's mother had the rare skill of being able to make a delicious meal with a few potatoes and a bit of lard. Lily would make sure she could do the same when she came into her dowry. She would ensure ten pounds was sufficient. She needn't ever depend on anyone else but herself once she turned twenty-five. She could make it four more years. She blinked and realized her own concerns had imposed themselves over her memories. It was time to get back to work. This house party wouldn't run itself.

Running through the servants' corridor and up the stairs, Lily slipped into Lester's library with the intention of checking to make sure the footmen had set it all to rights after what was sure to have been a rousing evening the night before.

She was shocked to encounter the handsome visiting earl rummaging through Lester's desk.

"What are you doing?" Her tone was censorious, as though she were speaking to one of the servants, rather than one of the nobles. Lily felt her colour rising but ignored it. She was out of practice speaking to the nobility, but it didn't matter. This man should not be going through Lester's things, no matter how repulsive Lester might be. He was still the master of this house, and his desk was to be left untouched by anyone but Lester and his steward.

The earl bumped his head as he jerked it up to gaze at her. He blinked. For a split second Lily thought she read consternation on his face, but within the space of his blink it was gone, and she thought she must have imagined the expression. His face relaxed into a befuddled grin.

"Good morning, Lady Violet's niece, perhaps you could help me. I'm looking for some paper. I need to have my servants send some more clothes. Didn't expect to stay here quite this long, you know?"

It seemed to be a reasonable request, but Lily found her suspicions remained high. When the earl had first looked at her when she had entered the room, she didn't sense any drunkenness in him. Now, the longer he talked, the more foxed he appeared. It was an unusual situation. In her experience, men became less inebriated, not more, with the passage of time. But looking for paper was a plausible reason to be digging in Lester's desk, she supposed.

"Was there none in your room? I could have sworn I just restocked the escritoire in the room you're staying in before your arrival."

The earl blinked again and colour touched his cheekbones. "I didn't even think to look there," he admitted sheepishly.

Lily smiled, charmed into relaxing slightly. She made her way around the large desk, reaching into the cabinet behind to find a few sheets of paper for the man.

"There's ink and a fresh pen in your room, too, if you'd like to write your message there." She didn't want to leave the man in Lester's library. It wasn't as though Lester did work in there, but it didn't seem right in some way. She felt uneasy in the earl's presence. It seemed as though he saw more than he ought. Even though he seemed to be worse for drink, she still felt as though he were studying her. And she needed to get out of that room. She didn't expect Lester to rise before noon, but then she hadn't expected to find the earl up and about either. If Lester found her in his library, he'd have the servants escort her out of Ashburn Place before she could even pack a bag.

Trying not to tap her toe with impatience, she stifled her reaction as the earl sat down at Lester's desk.

"I'm likely to forget by the time I get back to my room," he answered with a wry smile. "Since there's paper and ink right here, I'll just get it over with and off before it slips my mind again."

"Wouldn't that be dreadful?" Lily asked, allowing the irony to drip in her tone. She was torn. She didn't want to leave him there, but she needed to be elsewhere. Even with her distraction, she had been able to ascertain that the room had already been set to rights by the servants, so she didn't have any need to be there. It was unlikely too that the earl would do any damage unless he spilled the ink or something. She doubted Lester would actually mind the man using his desk. She conceded defeat.

"Ring if you need anything," she said as she backed from the room. She needed to get on with the rest of her duties.

Chapter Four

Brock blew out a sigh of relief. That young woman saw too much. *And why is she always everywhere watching?* It was the strangest situation. She was the viscount's stepmother's niece. She should be a guest of the house, not one of its servants. Brock would be relieved when he was done with this business. He couldn't stand the viscount, and Brock was becoming too concerned about his dealings with Lester's family connections. Brock couldn't allow his concerns to interfere with his own plans. He needed to finish his investigation and get out of Ashburn Place. His own estates needed his undivided attention.

As he searched, he kept his ears trained on the door, but his mind kept wanting to drift to thoughts of Lester's... what was she, his cousin? Step cousin? Was that a word? Whatever she was, she shouldn't be on his mind. She was a beautiful distraction. But his analytical mind couldn't refrain from wondering why she was acting as the steward and housekeeper of this large house when there were clearly others that ought to be filling those roles.

His focus sharpened when he found what appeared to be a promising lead, but he was filled with disappointment to realize it was merely a receipt for payment. It had caught his eye because previously, all he had found were bills. Clearly the viscount had been overspending. But this was not unusual amongst the *ton* and was not worth his time to consider. It had nothing to do with his investigation.

Minutes later, he had still found nothing. His mind returned to the receipt he had found. Brock dug back through the desk and found it again. It was so unusual, maybe he SHOULD look into it a bit further. Since he hadn't found anything else, he slipped it into his pocket. And just in time, too. Someone was coming. Brock began humming to himself and quickly scrawled out the letter he had assured the niece he had needed to write. He really needed to find out that young woman's name.

Brock grinned to himself. His mind hadn't been this divided in years, maybe not ever. It was unusual for him to fixate on anything when he was in the middle of an investigation. Maybe his mind was trying to tell him something. Maybe he needed to investigate HER. Brightening, he quickly wrote out another letter to be included in his first, directed to his overseer at the Home Office. If they had anything on her, they would send it to him. Encrypted of course, which would make it all the more interesting.

There were aspects to this job that he would definitely miss. The parts that used his mind were the most enjoyable. Pawing through a man's desk was the least. Pretending to be someone else was also a trial, but not so bad. Everyone pretended, at least to a certain degree. He didn't see anything dishonourable in acting like a drunken souse when he had only had one glass, or feigning interest in whatever useless topic the viscount was droning on about. But searching a man's private papers struck him as dishonourable. Of course, if the man was a traitor, he didn't deserve any honour, Brock reminded himself as he wracked his brain for where else to look. If the man was involved in the plot, there had to be proof of it somewhere. Lester wasn't smart enough to hide it this well.

The approaching person had passed without even glancing into the library. It must have been a servant. The niece would have wanted to verify that he had finished and not created a mess. But she was probably too busy elsewhere to trouble herself with his whereabouts. Or so he hoped. He didn't enjoy her searching gaze attaching itself to him. It made him feel like she could see right through to his soul. And that she saw everything, including his suspicions about her cousin. He wondered if she would help him if he explained everything to her. Surely she couldn't harbour any warm feelings toward the man.

Brock pushed the thought away. It would only complicate things, and he wanted this mission to be as uncomplicated as possible. He wanted out, he reminded himself. Getting an innocent young female involved would definitely complicate things. And he shouldn't need any help. This was certainly not the first large estate he had searched. Its size shouldn't matter. Brock just needed to focus on the matter and figure out where the viscount would have left anything incriminating.

Maybe he already had it. Maybe the receipt really did have significance. Since he hadn't been able to find anything else of import, Brock glanced around to ensure everything was exactly as he had found it. He scribbled on and crumpled up a couple of papers to lend credence to the length of time he had been in there. Then he went in search of the butler to send his letters home before returning to his room to study the receipt. He was grasping at straws, but he had nothing else to do. Even the estate ledgers hadn't been in the library. Brock was going to have to search the steward's room and office. That was going to be even trickier.

Lily watched the earl climb the stairs. His humming was surprisingly melodious for someone seemingly worse for drink. Wasn't it rather early to be drunk already? Or late? It wasn't even noon. When had he been drinking? Still the effects from last night, or had the man already started on the ale this morning? What a strange man. Lily couldn't stand the taste of most alcohols, so she couldn't understand the male preoccupation with drinking to excess. Did they really enjoy turning into bumbling idiots? It would seem so, since Lester and his friends did it so frequently. If they didn't enjoy it, surely they wouldn't do it. It wasn't like bathing. Whether you enjoyed it or not, you had to do it, but no one ever bathed to excess.

But this man seemed different from Lester's usual friends. There were times when Lily thought she had seen a gleam of intelligence in his gaze while he looked around the room. And occasionally she thought she had seen wry amusement in his features while he was with Lester's friends. But then it would disappear as though wiped off with a sponge. Lily was beginning to think the man was an imposter. He would bear watching, that was for certain. Lily actually thought she ought to warn someone about the man, but who? Lester didn't want her around at all; he certainly wouldn't welcome her suspicions about one of his guests. Aunt Violet would think she was being ridiculous and would want to take away her books, saying her imagination was running away with her. The steward might be able to keep his eye on things but wouldn't have any authority to do anything. Once again, Lily wished Uncle Wilbur hadn't died. He would've known what to do. Of course, if he was there, she wouldn't be in this situation at all. He had been well in control of his estates. Oh, he had allowed Lily to take an interest when she had first arrived, so bereft and at loose ends. But he had most definitely been the lord of his manor.

Lily was grateful that Uncle Wilbur had taught her the ins and outs of running the estates, though, otherwise, where would they all be now? Aunt Violet had never seen to it, and Lester refused to do so. Lily would have to teach Violet as much as she could before she left. Lily couldn't care less if Lester ran himself into the ground, but she didn't want her aunt left destitute due to his mismanagement. Of course, the steward seemed to be a reasonable man, but Violet needed to know what was what in order to be able to keep an eye on things. Lily was of the strong opinion that ignoring it didn't make things go away, for the most part. But when it came to money, it could very well be true. If you ignored it, it could disappear on you.

She didn't mind the work here at Ashburn Place. In fact, she quite liked it. She considered it to be her advanced education. It would serve her well when she finally received her ten pounds and was able to set up her bakery. Of course, it was all on a much grander scale here at the Place, but the principles would remain true. Watch your pennies, and the pounds could watch themselves. Treat your contacts with respect, and they would do the same. It would be heavenly. No one to watch over her. No one to resent her presence. Any profit would be hers to enjoy. She could barely wait.

All she had to do was get through the next four years. She really needed to get on with finding herself another position. The limbo she was in here at Ashburn was too grating on her nerves. Always wondering when Lester would finally throw her out on her ear. If she wasn't prepared, she could find herself in a very awkward position. She understood that Aunt Violet didn't want her to leave, but she needed to secure herself somewhere before Lester made his final move. She would discuss it with her aunt again soon.

But she supposed it would have to wait until the end of the house party. It would be beyond churlish to throw this at her aunt once more before the guests had even left. But, on the other hand, since her aunt didn't go about very much in Society since Wilbur's death, this might be the best opportunity to ask around whether anyone knew of a family looking for a governess or a companion.

Lily chewed her lip as she slowly climbed the stairs. Hearing footsteps coming toward her, she suddenly realized she was on the grand staircase and might be seen by anyone. She turned on her heel and ran back to the bottom. Not only was she not dressed for company, if it got back to Lester that she had been seen, she would be out on her ear without a moment to blink.

Heaving a sigh, Lily reached the servants' stairs and hurried up to her room. She ought to at least be properly dressed if she were going to be mingling at all. She should've ensured she had a uniform like the maids. Violet wouldn't hear of it, but it would have made her position a fair bit easier. No one would bat an eyelash to see another servant about. But since she was neither servant nor guest, she stood out awkwardly. Lily sighed and combed out her curls. She would stop in and check on her aunt before returning to the dining room to ensure the luncheon preparations were on track. The day was getting away from her. She had spent far too much time thinking about the handsome earl. That would not do. But she wondered why he was so stuck in her head. Lester had been inviting friends home ever since she had met him, and none of them had ever appealed to her. Until now. It was the strangest thing.

Some of his friends had even been exceedingly handsome. But their propensity for drinking and grabbing the maids had been enough to mar their beauty. But this earl was different. Even though he seemed to drink to excess, he never tripped over his feet and his eyes retained their clarity. It made it difficult for her to see him as a bumbling idiot. And her heart skipped a beat whenever she encountered him. Which was ridiculous, she reminded herself. She needn't get any such ideas. There was no room in her bakery plans for a handsome earl.

"Good morning, my darling," Aunt Violet called out as soon as Lily scratched on her door.

Lily entered the room, laughing. "What if it was one of the maids with your chocolate?"

"Well, if it was someone bearing chocolate, I would be inclined to call them darling, too," the countess answered with a twinkle. "But you are never late. It is exactly the time that you stop in to check on me every morning. Now, come over here and tell me what you have been doing."

Lillian wasn't sure if her aunt really wanted to know all the mundane tasks she had seen to, but she told her a little bit of it.

"The housekeeper is still under the weather, poor soul. I'm wondering if we ought to call in the doctor to see her."

"Does she want him called?"

"Of course not."

Violet laughed. "Well then, wait and see a couple more days. I know it's unfortunate timing, but we'll manage."

Lily smiled. Of course "they" would. She managed not to roll her eyes at her aunt's words. "The kitchen is well stocked and prepared to manage the rest of the party. Everyone IS leaving by the end of the week, though, right?"

"Oh, yes, no worries there. The Marquis of Abernathy is hosting a summer fete on his estate. Most of the nobility will be heading in his direction by Saturday."

"Are you planning to go?"

"No." Violet's answer was succinct with little inflection.

"Why not? You said everyone was going."

"No, I said most were going. I have no interest in being with that crowd without my Wilbur. If I were escorting you, it would be a different matter, but as it stands, I know I wouldn't enjoy it."

Lily felt a spasm of worry for her aunt. She had seemed to love the socialising of the Season while her husband was alive.

"Are you enjoying Lester's house party?" Lily tried to get to the root of her aunt's feelings.

"It isn't nearly as bad as I had expected. Of course, I know a great deal of the reason is because you are doing everything I ought to be. But the people he invited, or rather the chaperones of the people he invited, aren't nearly as insipid as I had expected."

They shared a giggle over this. "The young ladies are a trifle vapid, though, aren't they?"

"What would you expect if they accepted an invitation from Lester?"

"They are very young. And he is a viscount. They may not have realized what he is. And he has been on remarkably good behaviour, I must say. He and his friends confine most of their messy drinking to his library. I can't believe I'm saying this, but it was actually a good idea that they invited ladies to join them. I think even such halfwits as Lester and his friends have been raised from the cradle to treat ladies a certain way. They cannot counteract that breeding so easily. Despite the work of all the extra people, it isn't so very bad to have a house full."

"Am I allowing you to work too hard? I really shouldn't let you take it all on. Why don't you make me bestir myself?"

Lily was torn with consternation. Part of her realized she shouldn't allow her aunt to wallow in her grieving. But she was honest enough to admit, "I like the control, Aunt Violet. I wish I could be a housekeeper. I find I really enjoy running a household like this. Or a steward! That would be the best. But of course, no one is going to hire a gently bred woman to be their steward. Nor their housekeeper, either."

"Oh, Lillian, I wish you weren't so bent on finding yourself a position."

"Well, I can't really stay here comfortably, can I, Aunt? Since Lester has made it so clear how unwelcome I am, it's only a matter of time before he follows through on his threats, don't you think?"

"I think he just enjoys threatening. I don't really think he's so very bad that he would throw you out for real."

Lily grinned. "But that's just because you always see the best in everyone. And you don't want to think that I'll do something to rile him up and make him throw me out."

Lady Violet's eyes rounded. "Would you really do that?"

"Well not on purpose, of course. But he's just so very easy to rile, especially when he's in his cups. Of course, if, as you said, everyone is going to Abernathy, we shall have a respite from him for a while. Then he'll surely go up to London for the Season, so we probably needn't worry overly about him for a couple months after this. But I do think I ought to get myself sorted sooner rather than later. I need the next four years to be occupied, and I would rather not have to be looking over my shoulder for Lester's wrath for the duration of them."

"Oh, my darling niece, don't you realize, you'll be looking over your shoulder for someone anyway if you take a position. You are gentry. And beautiful. It won't be a comfortable situation for you whether it is here or elsewhere. I would much prefer keeping you here."

"But if I was elsewhere, I could at least draw a wage." Lily winced over her aunt's pained expression.

"Yes, of course, I had forgotten about that. Perhaps I could share my pin money with you."

"Aunt Violet, that is a generous offer, but you know you haven't been left so very much. That is the entire reason for Lester's threats. You don't have enough to support me, and he refuses to do so. Yes, I could try to stay here for the next four years, but I will be no further ahead financially. If I find a position, I will at least have a little bit to add to the ten pounds that I will receive when I turn twenty-five."

The viscountess' gaze turned uncharacteristically shrewd. "Do you really suppose ten pounds is going to set you up in your bakery, Lillian? That really isn't very much money."

"It's all in your perspective, my lady." Lily's answer was a little stiff at first, but then she continued. "I know, I've seen the books here, ten pounds is spent easily on anything in a place like this. But yes, I've done the budget, and I've priced things out. Ten pounds will set me up just fine. Well, provided prices don't rise exorbitantly in the next four years. That is why it would be so very helpful if I was to gain a little more money in the meantime."

Lady Violet sighed. "Very well. I will do my best to help you. I may not know anyone who might hire you, but I know someone who knows everyone. Lady Mortimer will help you. I will write to her when this party is over."

Lillian squeezed her aunt in a warm hug. "Thank you, Aunt Violet. I know it would be more comfortable for me to stay here, but I need to think to my future."

"I know, my dear, I just wished for a different future for you."

Lily couldn't restrain her amusement. "Perhaps I will meet the love of my life while I'm serving some noblewoman elsewhere."

The countess smiled and brightened. "That's a possibility, I suppose. Yes, I will ask Lady Mortimer to help you find a position as companion rather than governess. There's no chance of meeting someone suitable if you're a governess."

"You never know. There might be some poor, lonely widower needing a governess for his motherless children."

Ever the romantic, the countess didn't notice the sarcasm hidden in Lily's tone. "That's true. Oh, I don't know what's best." She concluded on a tone close to a wail.

Lily giggled. "My dearest aunt, don't worry about it. Tell Lady Mortimer my qualifications and ask her if she knows of any suitable position. If she knows everyone who's anyone, she'll know what's best."

"Do you really think so? You're so very brave to be even considering it. If I were you, I think I would remain huddled in my bed all day every day."

Lily grinned. "Lester might've liked me more if I had done so, I suppose. But that would have been dreadful. I am not one to huddle. And I really doubt that you are either. Just look at you – playing hostess to your ogre of a stepson and all his ridiculous friends."

"Do you really think they're ridiculous?"

Lily quirked her eyebrows at her aunt, and Lady Violet quickly agreed. "Well, yes, of course, most of them are rather silly, but what about that handsome earl, Sedgwick? He doesn't strike me as quite the same as the others."

"No, you're right, he doesn't to me either. But I don't know about him. There seems to be something shady about him. I meant to ask you, do you have a copy of Debrett's handy? I wanted to read up on his earldom."

"Why Lillian, are you interested in the earl?"

Lily went off in a gale of laughter. When she finally gained control of herself and wiped her eyes, she thanked her aunt. "I really needed that laugh, thank you so much. But, no, I am not interested in him in any sort of romantic way. I just find him suspicious. I want to make sure he is who he says he is. Debrett's will have the listing of births and deaths of the earls. If he doesn't seem to be the right age, I'll know he's an imposter."

She strolled toward the small shelf where her aunt's few books were kept. Sure enough, there was the volume with the listing of the various aristocratic families. It was a little out of date, but that was just as well. She would be able to tell if the man claiming to be Sedgwick seemed authentic.

The countess blinked at her niece, at a momentary loss for words. It quickly passed. "An imposter? But people recognize him."

"Do they really? Or was he just about during the Season and everyone has accepted him? How long have you known him?"

"What has gotten into you? I'm fairly certain I've known the earl for years, but now that you're asking me questions, I cannot actually say for certain. Being a younger man, he wasn't really one of Wilbur's cronies. But everyone at the party seems quite familiar with him."

Lily made a noncommittal humming noise, not willing to accept that there was nothing questionable about the earl. She was certain there was. Thumbing through the book, she finally arrived at the entry for the Sedgwick earldom. Putting her finger in the volume to hold her place, Lily looked back up at her aunt, trying to explain.

"He watches everything and sees too much."

Violet grinned. "What is that supposed to mean?"

"All the other nobles only see what they want to see. No one sees me, for one thing." She hastened to add when Violet was about to protest, "Not that I mind, I assure you. They all seem rather dreadful. I don't know how you manage to make conversation with them all day. But he sees everything."

"Just like you do, my dear. Perhaps you'd be a perfect match."

This set Lily off into another fit of laughter. "I love you, my darling aunt. You are tenacious, if nothing else. Never mind about trying to make matches. I should let you dress, and I need to make sure the dining room is set up and ready for the afternoon nuncheon. Everyone who wanted to break their fast in the dining room has already been up for some time now."

Lily turned her attention back to the book in her hands. Disappointment filled her as she read the entry. According to the older version of Debrett's, the second son of the Earl of Sedgwick was Brock Chadwick Marwood Ralston, born August 23, 1779. Viscount Marwood, the earl's firstborn was Chester Francis George Ralston. That fit as she had heard her aunt mention the earl and his heir had died in some sort of boating accident. She heaved a sigh of disappointment. This didn't prove anything either way. It could fit. Or he could be anyone. It wasn't as though the book held a description of the man. He probably hadn't even reached his majority when the volume had been printed. She slid the book back onto the shelf and turned to leave.

"Before you go, do you really think we should call the doctor for Mrs. Parker?" Violet called to her.

"The poor, stubborn dear refuses. Her leg is improving, but she is still not able to get around much."

Violet chewed her lip, indecision clearly written across her face. "Perhaps I ought to hire someone else. It just isn't right for you to be doing her work."

"You could hire me," Lily replied with aplomb, a big grin stretching her face. "That would solve our problems nicely."

"Lillian Susanna Shaw. You know I couldn't do that. You should be a member of the family, not a member of the staff."

Lily kept her smile in place as she stepped from the room. *Maybe I should be, but I'm sort of both at the moment.* Getting paid would make it a little nicer. And maybe Lester would be less antagonistic if she were a member of the staff. He would feel she had been properly put in her place if she were a staff member. Of course, poor Aunt Violet was still holding on to hope that she could marry Lily to a nobleman. That would be out of the question if she were to become a paid staff member. But how is it any different if she becomes a businesswoman? That, no doubt, was why the viscountess was fighting Lily's decision so fiercely.

Aunt Violet considered that it would be beyond the pale. Not that it mattered. Lily didn't have any intention of marrying anyone, nobleman or not. From what she could tell, a husband was nothing but trouble. A nobleman more so than anyone else. Just look at Aunt Violet's situation. Yes, she was a viscountess, but along with that came a nasty stepson who gave her nothing but trouble and a huge house for which to be responsible.

With her simple background, she hadn't been prepared to take on such a task. While Uncle Wilbur had been alive, it hadn't mattered much. The staff at Ashburn Place were well trained and everything functioned smoothly. But with the passage of time, things change and a firmer hand than sweet Aunt Violet could exert was needed. Lily, brought into this house at a younger age and with a much more inquiring mind, had been trained by Uncle Wilbur and was able to keep things flowing, but it wasn't really a comfortable position for any of them to be in.

Uncle Wilbur had considered her to be the daughter he never had. If she truly had been his daughter, it would continue to be her place to run the household. The staff were used to following her orders as they had under Wilbur's direction, but everyone knew how precarious Lester made her position. Since he rejected her, it was awkward and uncomfortable. Not everyone was so interested in listening to her any longer. Even the steward, who she had always considered her ally, was refusing to meet with her. Lillian hoped it was merely his male pride speaking and not any actual problems with the estate.

Lily knew wasn't really her place to be running the household, especially since Lester had made it clear that she wasn't welcome. If he had acknowledged her as a family member, she would happily run the household and the current awkwardness wouldn't exist. But as things were, she only remained because of her aunt, though she wouldn't be able to do that much longer. Lily would need to ensure her aunt wrote that promised letter.

But first, the dining room needed to be overseen.

"No, no, William, we need two more chairs. From what I understand from Mr. Johnson, another earl and his daughter arrived late last night and will be joining the rest for nuncheon."

It was a brief flurry of activity before everything was just as she wanted it. With a nod of satisfied approval, Lily admired the finished product. Of course, their noble guests would have it destroyed within minutes, but she was happy with the work they had accomplished. Everything was in its place and ready for the meal to be served. Each setting was exactly correct. The staff was perfectly trained.

Lily smiled her thanks as the footmen drifted back to the kitchens, prepared to return when the bell was rung to serve the meal. It was time for Lillian to make herself scarce. Lester's guests would be milling about soon. She too made her way down to the kitchen. She knew it made the cook uncomfortable if she spent too much time there, but she was hungry, and it was the only way for her to get fed. She didn't want to spare one of the maids from waiting on the guests just to serve her.

"It smells heavenly in here, as always, Cook," Lily called out as she entered the high strung Frenchman's domain. He shot her a distracted smile. Lily was not deceived. The man was as sharp as a tack. She and Violet met weekly with the man. Nothing got past him that had anything to do with the feeding of the large household. She had been meeting with him briefly each day since the start of Lester's house party to ensure they were fully stocked and everything was running smoothly. Even though he too was unsure about Lily's place in the household, she loved visiting his small office with all the hanging herbs he was forever drying. It smelt exactly how she imagined a spice emporium would smell. Lily grinned. She was being fanciful, but she wished she had the freedom to travel to the lands where truly exotic spices originated. She imagined it would smell heavenly.

She would have an herb garden behind her bakery, she resolved. She would bake savoury breads besides the sweets she planned to produce. Her baked goods would be the most popular baked items for several counties around the small hamlet where she was going to set up. The exaggerated reverie kept the grin in place as she accepted the plate of food a footman offered her. She slipped into the servants' hall and found a quiet corner to eat. Her position of limbo made everyone uncomfortable. She was glad the room was almost empty so she needn't discomfit too many in her efforts to keep herself nourished.

Making quick work of emptying her plate, Lily allowed her mind to drift in fantasizing about the bakery she wanted to open. It was rather strange that this was her goal in life, when one considered her circumstances. If her parents hadn't died and if Uncle Wilbur hadn't died, she probably would have had a London Season as befitted a young woman born into the gentry. But those things did happen. And even before her parents had died, they had periodically joked about her opening a bakery. She and her mother had always loved to spend time together in the kitchen. Lily's mother had been an exceptionally good cook, but Lily had exceeded her in the baking department. They'd had grand times inventing new recipes, usually to the delight of everyone around them, but occasionally they'd had their failures. Lily's mother had always laughed it off. "That is how you learn," she'd say as they served the concoction to the pigs. The animals never complained.

It was the bequest that would make her dream possible. Dear Mr. Byram. He had left his small fortune to the town of Sherton and had decreed that a portion of it was to be divided up, and ten pounds was to be endowed upon each impoverished young woman who had grown up in Sherton as a dowry. His intention had been to make the young women more marriageable, but he had kindly made it possible to access the money upon the age of twenty-five, even if she were to remain single. That was Lily's intention. She was going to achieve her goals on her own merit; she didn't need a husband to do it for her. And she certainly didn't need to aspire to marriage as her one goal in life.

Thinking of the silly young ladies who were included in Lester's house party set Lily's teeth on edge and curbed her appetite. Their one goal was to ensnare one of the noblemen as a husband. The wealthier or better born, the better, of course.

Lily had heard a group of ladies discussing the gentlemen in the green salon two days before as she had passed by the room on her way to confer with the housekeeper about one of the bedchambers. They had been giggling over Mr. Sheffield's income.

"I've heard it's as much as ten thousand pounds a year." This had been uttered in tones of awe.

"But it doesn't come with a coronet," pointed out one of the others with a disappointed air.

"One could buy several coronets with ten thousand pounds," had tittered another.

Lily had rolled her eyes. Yes, ten thousand pounds was a staggering amount of money, but what of his personality? She had observed Mr. Sheffield. For one thing, the fact that he was a friend of Lester put him in her black books, but she had also seen the way he treated the servants. Lily had been forced to rearrange the staffing in the wing of the house in which Mr. Sheffield had been roomed. Only footmen were on duty there. None of the maids were to be left alone with the man. Lily was certain if the man would so mistreat a servant, he shouldn't be trusted with a wife, either.

She was well aware that members of the nobility considered the servants beneath them and would probably treat their wives differently than how they treated their servants, but it went to character. If he could so mistreat another human, she doubted he would be sweet and kind to his wife. Especially if she were to overspend her pin money, as Lily knew noblewomen were wont to do. She had overheard several conversations about that, as well.

"I'm shattered until the next quarter."

"Couldn't you ask for an advance on your next quarter?"

"I don't intend to tell my guardian the situation. He'll want to know what I spent it on."

The laughter that had followed made Lily certain the young woman wasn't to be trusted. It only reinforced her view of the nobility. Of course, she had met some lovely specimens of the gentry and even nobles. Uncle Wilbur had been the best. He had introduced her to a few of his friends who had also seemed quite pleasant. But they all lived in a different world from the rest of reality. Lily was definitely a creature of the real world.

Her parents had died when she was seventeen. The flu that had taken them had just barely spared her. She had been weak and exhausted from illness and grief when Aunt Violet had brought her to stay at Ashburn Place. The viscount and his wife had been kind, loving, and patient with her during her convalescence and grieving. It had been fortunate that Lester had been away at school and had barely visited. Lily had finally regained her strength and joined the household.

During her illness, when she had been well enough, Wilbur had allowed her to sit with him while he was meeting with the steward. It had been the highlight of her weeks. She had loved the mathematics involved. And the tidiness of it all. If she had been a man, she would have been a clerk, for sure. One column had to add up and match the other column. It was perfect and precise. Of course, the steward and Uncle Wilbur thought it was a bit of a joke, but Lily had taken the accounts deadly seriously. And now she needed to impress their importance upon her aunt. She couldn't, in good faith, leave the household until her aunt could fully understand how the books worked. It was for her own protection.

Lily didn't trust Lester any farther than she could throw him. She wouldn't put it past him to change the steward to one who wouldn't have Ashburn's interests at his heart. Lily knew Uncle Wilbur had trusted Ralph to run his estate. They had seemed to have a good working relationship, and the man was very knowledgeable about all aspects of running Ashburn. Even though Ralph would no longer answer her questions, Lily was sure the steward would have no qualms in telling Lester if he was overdrawing on the estate. It hadn't come to that, yet. It appeared to Lily that they were still profitable. But with how extravagantly Lester liked to live, she couldn't trust that things would remain so smooth. And if the steward ever had to try to exercise some restraint upon Lester, things could get very ugly. So, to protect the viscountess and her financial stake in Ashburn Place, Lady Violet needed to know how things worked. Lillian felt it was her responsibility to see to that education for her beloved aunt.

Chapter Five

V iolet found herself glancing into a mirror as she passed it in the salon and then reprimanded herself for such vanity. Just because the handsome Lord Avery had arrived did not give her leave to lose her sensibility. But she hadn't expected the handsome earl to be present at Lester's party, and she couldn't prevent the girlish thrill that assailed her at the thought of spending a couple days in the older gentleman's company.

When Lillian had told her they would be arriving today, it had taken all her skills not to betray her interest in the subject. As it was, just thinking about her attraction to the earl filled Violet with guilt. Her darling husband had barely been gone more than a year. She couldn't believe she was eager to see another man. Not that anything would come of it, of course. She had no interest in remarrying. Not that Lord Avery would even consider her for the role of his next countess, of course, she reminded herself.

Violet shook her head. She was being unforgivably foolish. Her steps faltered for a moment as a thought struck her. If she did remarry, she would be in a position to provide for Lillian far better than she was in her current situation at Lester's mercy. Of course, she had been provided for sufficiently, but not enough to also provide for Lillian. Perhaps it would behove her to consider remarriage.

Sure, Violet, keep telling yourself your motives are purely altruistic, she thought to herself with uncharacteristic sarcasm. *At least be honest in your own head.* Violet ignored her disquieting thoughts. She had guests to attend.

"Good morning," she called to the assembled guests. There was a rustle of activity as various people acknowledged her greeting. The couple of gentlemen present made to rise to their feet, but Violet quickly waved them back to their seats with a grateful smile. "I'm pleased to see you're being well cared for."

"You have very well trained servants, my lady."

Violet dipped her chin in what she knew would appear to be gracious acknowledgement of the woman's words, but she squirmed inwardly. So much of the running of her household was being looked after by her niece. It was a state of affairs she couldn't allow to continue. The darling girl ought to be enjoying her life, not working herself into an early grave acting as an unpaid servant in this household. Presently, though, Violet didn't see a solution to the dilemma, and the rest of the house party needed to be gotten through. She would pursue her concerns next week.

Scanning the room, Violet spotted the newest addition to the household and rustled over to take a seat next to the young woman.

"Good morning, Lady Katherine. I'm pleased to see that you are no worse for your travels. My staff tells me you and your father arrived after I had retired for the evening. I trust they saw to your comfort sufficiently."

"Oh, yes, thank you for asking Lady Violet. We felt so badly about arriving that late."

"Did you run into difficulties on the road?"

"A broken wheel, can you believe it?"

Violet laughed. "Unfortunately I can, with the state of some of the roads. Were you terribly uncomfortable on the road?"

The young woman let out a tinkle of laughter. "It actually wasn't so dreadful. We were lucky enough to break down just as we were about to drive through a small village, so there was an inn I was able to easily walk to for refreshment while I waited. And of course, being so close to the village made the repairs much easier to accomplish. We were only held up a couple hours. It really wouldn't have been worth it to continue if the timing hadn't worked out."

"What do you mean?"

"Since my father would only agree for us to come to the very end of the party, if we weren't going to make it last night, we would have had to turn around and go home without bothering to come."

"Oh, that would have been just too bad."

"Wouldn't it?" the girl asked with another laugh. "I actually suspected my father had arranged for the breakdown just to prevent me from coming, but our driver and outriders were quick and skilled, so my plans didn't get spoiled at all."

Violet laughed along with the girl. "Do you really think your father has the ability to break your wheels from inside the carriage? That would be a dangerous proposition if it were true."

Katherine laughed again. "No, I was just disgruntled over the delay. I know he wouldn't do something like that. He isn't the sneaky sort. He would have just denied me outright to come, if he had really wanted to prevent it."

"Why wouldn't he want you to come to our party?"

Violet was surprised when the young woman blushed deeply and averted her gaze. Obviously, she hadn't meant to say anything about it and was embarrassed to have admitted as much.

"Oh, my lady, I meant no offence." The young woman stammered and blushed. Violet felt the need to comfort her even though she didn't understand what she meant.

"Of course, you didn't, and I assure you I took no offence. I'm just glad you made it and will be able to enjoy your time here."

Lady Katherine didn't seem convinced by Violet's words, and she appeared to want to share her thoughts even though Violet hadn't prodded for them. The younger woman leaned forward.

"My father thinks Lord Shepley is a reprobate and didn't want me to attend his party." Katherine uttered the words in a voice resonating with the thrill of doing the forbidden. Violet had to quell her amusement.

"Well, I cannot blame your father. Shepley *is* a reprobate, I'm fairly sure. But when he is at home he is careful not to go too far beyond the bounds of decency most of the time, so you needn't fear you'll be put to the blush."

Violet's amusement deepened when the girl appeared to be disappointed with her words.

"Have you seen your father yet this morning, my lady? Do you know if he is sufficiently recovered from yesterday's exertions?" Violet hadn't meant anything but solicitous concern with her question, but the younger woman laughed.

"My father never needs to recover from anything, my lady. He was up early and went for his usual ride before the rest of the household had stirred, I'm sure. I only saw him briefly. As I entered the breakfast room he was leaving with his cup of coffee. He said there was too much chatter there and he needed to find somewhere quiet to read his paper."

Violet smiled. "That's fine, then. I'm sure I shall encounter him at some point. I am delighted to hear you have settled in comfortably. Can I do anything to make your visit any more pleasant?"

"If it was any more pleasant, I don't know if I could stand it," the young woman exclaimed, her enthusiasm threatening to get out of hand.

Violet nodded and excused herself. She would need to remember to mention the young woman to Lillian. She would bear scrutiny to ensure she wasn't looking for trouble during her stay here at Ashburn. It was obvious to Violet that the lovely, young Lady Katherine was enamoured with the thought of spending time with a bunch of rakes, but Violet would not allow any young woman's ruination under her roof. If she thought he would listen, Violet would offer a warning to Lester as well. Stifling her sigh, Violet swept from the room.

She was passing the open door to the green room when she heard a faint rustle, which prompted Violet to stick her head into what she thought was an empty room. There was the earl himself folding his paper, presumably to make the page easier to read.

"Good morning, Lord Avery, I was just speaking with Lady Katherine. I was sorry to hear you had wheel trouble on the road."

"Good morning, my lady. Yes, what can one expect with the roads in such dreadful shape after the wet winter we had? We were grateful they were no longer swampy with mud, but our old wheels weren't up to the challenge of getting over the ruts and dips left behind."

"At least you weren't held up for too very long."

"No, it was merely a minor inconvenience. I was just surprised. Since you aren't so very far from London, I had expected the roads in these parts to be in better condition."

"I think the one blessing has resulted in a curse," Violet replied. Her mysterious answer caused the earl to raise an inquisitive eyebrow. Violet blushed and tried to explain. "We are blessed with many roads in the area, but that makes it more work to maintain, I would expect. And I don't think all the landowners in the area are so quick to get on with it."

"Well, I was impressed with the state of the roads closest to your lands."

Violet nodded. "Lil gave it priority as soon as it was dry enough but before it got too dry."

The earl's eyebrows seemed to question who "Lil" was, which Violet regretted, but he merely agreed, "That was wise, I'm sure."

Violet hurried to change the subject, wanting to be away from the handsome man and the way he could turn her head. "Have you been made comfortable by the servants, my lord? Can I do anything to make your stay more comfortable?"

His eyes narrowed, and Violet's blush deepened as she realized her words could be taken to imply a more intimate offer than the one she had meant. She thought of turning on her heel and leaving the man, but her good breeding kept her in place to brazen it out. The earl must have detected her discomfort because his face relaxed and creased into a warm smile.

"It would seem I have all that I need, I thank you, Lady Violet."

Violet was about to leave the room when her stride hitched, and she turned back to the earl. He was still watching her attentively, and she questioned the wisdom of what she wanted to ask him.

"Was there something else, my lady?" He asked the question as he rustled the pages of his newsprint. Violet wanted to shrink from the room but remembered that her honour was at stake. She cleared her throat delicately before asking her question.

"As I mentioned, I spoke with your daughter this morning."

"Yes," he prompted, a question mark in his voice.

"She mentioned you did not want to allow her to come because of my stepson's reputation. I do hope you realize I would not stand for underhanded behaviour while I am in residence."

The earl's gaze had gone from warm to glacial within the space of her first sentence.

"Really, my lady? How would you stop him? It does not seem to me that you have the strength to exert any control over the man."

Violet's colour rose along with her rarely roused ire. The fact that his words were true didn't make them any less hurtful or offensive.

"He might be a rake, my lord, but he has enough respect for his father's memory to keep such things away from me."

The earl inclined his head toward her in a form of acknowledgment that did nothing to set her at ease.

"You will note, my dear lady, that we are present, so you mustn't think that we think too ill of you."

Violet realized there was nothing to be gained from trying to discuss this with the earl. Really, what did she hope to gain? She questioned herself as she nodded and carried on her way. She needed to regain control of her affairs, she decided firmly and went in search of her niece.

"Can you even imagine the man's temerity?" she demanded.

Lillian's understanding smile did nothing to cool the temper that had still not subsided in Violet's heart. How could the man think so ill of her? And why did she care? This last question brought Violet up short. She was acting like a simpleton. While the thought of remarrying was unappealing and the thought of helping Lillian held great appeal, the fact remained that Violet respected Lord Avery and was hurt that he obviously did not return the sentiment.

They had enjoyed multiple brief conversations through the years of her marriage to the viscount. Violet's husband had considered the earl a friend. If she remembered correctly, they had gone to school together and had even spent some of their Grand Tour together. Violet had always enjoyed his quick wit and steady, calm personality whenever their paths had crossed. It had been a shame when his wife had died. She had been a lovely lady, as well. Not that Violet had known her all that well. She hadn't enjoyed the most robust health and had remained at home on their estate much of the time during the Season.

Lillian interrupted Violet's thoughts and pulled her from her wool gathering. "Don't let the man irk you, Aunt Vi. His opinion means nothing. It is your opinion of yourself which matters most. And you are well aware that you are a respectable lady and deserve to be recognized as such. If he doesn't wish to do so, that is his loss. The rest of the guests seem to be perfectly content with being here and have done nothing to make me think they are questioning the wisdom of accepting the invitation."

"But did you have any refusals when you sent out Lester's invitations? I didn't think to ask previously."

"Surprisingly, no," Lillian answered. "I had expected there to be at least a few refusals since people would already have had plans, or so I thought. But everyone accepted. Of course, Lady Katherine and Lord Avery replied that they could only come for the end of the party, but they were the only ones. Perhaps Lester had the sense not to ask that high sticklers be invited, but from what I know of the *ton*, no one of ill repute is on the guest list. If I didn't know better, I would have almost thought Lester was looking for a viscountess."

Violet looked at her niece, stunned by her words. "Do you really think so? I hadn't thought to become a dowager so soon."

Lillian laughed. "As I said, I know Lester better. I strongly doubt he is looking for a wife. He merely likes to stir up controversy. I'm sure he's well aware that some parents would have their doubts about bringing their daughters here. He probably wanted to see who would accept. He was no doubt just as surprised as I was."

Violet wasn't so sure about Lillian's opinion. She no longer felt settled in her home. She supposed she ought to have realized it was no longer her home once her husband died and her stepson inherited the title. But since she was so comfortable there with Lillian and their staff taking such wonderful care of things, she had become complacent. That needed to change. And perhaps she ought to actually consider the idea of remarrying. Not to Lord Avery, of course, no matter how handsome he was or how she used to enjoy his company. If the man didn't consider her suitable company for his daughter, he wasn't worth her wasting any thought on him.

She told herself that but then realized it was far easier said than done. The handsome gentleman seemed to have invaded her thoughts and was very difficult to dispel. Violet couldn't shake her irritation over his persistent residence in her mind. It was probably the fact that he so obviously disapproved of her, she reassured herself as she prepared for the evening meal. She couldn't help wondering what he would think of her in the modest, mauve gown. While she rather thought she was looking her best, she doubted anyone else would notice. A disconsolate sniff brought her to attention. She refused to allow one man's opinion to bring her to depression.

Violet resolved to speak to Lester about having a Season in order to find another husband for herself. She would phrase her request in such a way that he would see it was in his own best interests. And she would insist that she would require Lillian's company. Then Lester would sponsor Lillian for her Season as well. She couldn't understand why she hadn't thought of it before. She would discuss it with Lillian as soon as Lester's guests departed.

Thus settled in her mind, Violet felt much more confident about the remainder of the house party, even if the Averys were there. She sallied forth from her room with her head held high, no longer perturbed by her nagging thoughts.

Chapter Six

B rock left his room, disappointed that he hadn't been able to discover anything nefarious from the receipt he had found. Perhaps the viscount truly had just paid a bill. It happened. Brock himself never allowed his debts to pile up. His father had assured him he was most unnatural for doing so, but Brock didn't allow that to weigh with him. He figured the tradespeople he worked with deserved their pay. He couldn't imagine how difficult it must be to work for a living and wouldn't compound their challenges by not paying them. It wasn't as though he didn't have the money. He doubted the viscount was lacking in funds either. Ashburn Place, from what he could tell, was run quite efficiently and seemed to be productive. Of course, it cost a king's ransom to run a house like this, so it might not be as rosy at it appeared. Appearances could be deceptive; he knew that for certain. In his line of work, he had learned that no one was ever as they seemed.

Just take the viscountess' niece for example. She was the most contradictory creature he had yet come across. Beautiful in a very understated way with her hair all scraped back and dressed in plain, boring gowns. She should have been attending the house party as one of the guests. Surely she was gentry, even if she wasn't a noblewoman. But it would appear that she was running the household. She never sat still long enough for him to actually get a good read on her thoughts or feelings, but she didn't seem to be working under duress.

Brock had only seen her talking with her aunt once, but there had seemed to be genuine warmth in their interaction. Besides, Lady Violet was one of the sweetest women Brock had ever met, so he couldn't envision her enslaving her niece under any pretext. And Lester, for all his debauchery, didn't have the power to enslave her, unless he was holding something over her. But from their brief encounter, he also doubted the young woman would stand for any abuse of herself. She seemed perfectly capable of putting anyone in their place should they have the misguided notion of trying to take advantage of her.

Unless she had indentured herself, Brock thought for a moment. It was possible she was working to support her family. He knew many of the gentry could find themselves in tight spots if their lands weren't extensive enough to support a large family or the father had losses at the table. Perhaps her aunt had hired her assistance as a favour. Brock still didn't like the thought of the young woman working so hard and not enjoying what she was owed as a matter of her birth, but it wasn't really his place to even have an opinion.

Once again, he realized he needed to dismiss the lovely young woman from his mind. This mission was the hardest he'd ever been on, and he had been in some dangerous positions before. But he had never had to work so hard to keep his focus. It was distraction that could get a man killed. Not that he truly believed he was in any kind of danger here at Ashburn Place, but it was the principle of the matter.

What is it about this girl that has gotten under my skin? He had seen more beautiful women in the past. He had met people with far more difficult circumstances. And he knew many more intelligent people, both men and women. But she seemed to be a combination of all of those. Beautiful, intelligent, and obviously in need. It brought out every protective instinct he possessed, and it was only his mission that prevented him from seeking her out and trying to set her situation to rights. Well, his mission and his goals. He needed to finish this mission to achieve his goal of a quiet life settled in on his estates. Sedgwick was calling him home. It had been too long since he had felt settled anywhere.

Before he was able to accomplish the task of forgetting about the lovely young woman, he came across her in the hallway. She was carrying a large crate.

"Let me help you with that," he exclaimed as he hurried to take it from her hands.

"I've got it."

She didn't seem particularly delighted by his offer of help, but Brock ignored her implied objection and held on tightly to the crate. She must have realized it would be ridiculous to struggle to retain her hold on it, so she let go. Brock was surprised as the full weight came to bear in his arms. She was surprisingly strong for such a slight woman.

"Where would you like this?" he asked. While he was a strong man, he was amazed at how heavy the crate was and wouldn't be disappointed to deposit it somewhere.

"The ballroom," she answered simply. Brock was almost certain the ballroom was at the other side of the large house. He stifled a groan.

"How did you manage to carry this? You're just a wisp of a thing."

Her soft chuckle shot directly to his midsection, making him weak. For a moment, he thought he would have to hand the crate back to her.

"For one thing, I'm obviously much tougher than I appear. I'm not so very wispy. And for another, I've been carrying heavier and heavier items for years."

Brock wanted to put his burden down and question her further. And it wasn't just because the blasted thing was heavy. He was overwhelmed with curiosity about the young woman.

"Why have you been building up your stamina in this way?"

She chuckled again. "It wasn't an intentional exercise. Necessity is the mother of all invention, they say. I needed to carry heavier items, so I did."

"You aren't very old. Where were your parents?" He was probably stepping beyond the realms of polite conversation, but he couldn't help himself, and she didn't seem to be offended.

"They weren't well, unfortunately. My mother was the loveliest woman you would ever lay your eyes on. But she was sickly from my birth."

"I'm sorry." Brock now felt awkward for asking and wished he could change the subject. He was surprised by her matter of fact attitude and almost startled when she shrugged.

"It does sound tragic, but it was all that I knew. And she always seemed so happy despite her weak health. The greatest tragedy is that she finally succumbed to that weakness."

"What about your father?" Brock hated the compulsion to pursue his questions but was relieved that she didn't appear to mind.

"He didn't seem to be able to cope without my mother. They were the dreamiest people you would ever meet. I'm not sure where they found me. I'm probably the most practical person you'll ever come across. If I didn't look so much like my parents, I would think I was a changeling."

Brock's laughter surprised them both and once again weakened his arms. He was beginning to find the awkward load more than burdensome. Feeling heat fill his face, he finally stopped and placed it on the floor at his feet.

"I'm sorry, I don't know how you managed it, but I need to stop for a moment."

The urchin by his side let out another husky chuckle.

"I'm actually impressed with how far you managed without a break. I was needing to stop about every ten feet when I was carrying it."

Brock felt his eyebrows rising into his hairline. "Then why were you carrying such a burden? Why not enlist one of the footmen?"

She shrugged. "Because I'm as stubborn as a goat and didn't realize how very heavy I had filled the blasted crate, nor how awkward it was to fit my arms around, until I had already set out with it. By then, my stubborn nature had taken over and there was no way I was going to admit that it was too hard for me." She paused for a moment before offering him a shy but sly smile. "Then you came across me and your gentlemanly offer of assistance wasn't deniable."

Brock laughed. "You just wanted to see me fail, didn't you?"

"Have you failed?" she asked. "You carried it far further than I had thought you would manage, and you didn't even complain. Rather you apologized as though you felt badly for holding me up. You are quite unexpected for an earl."

Brock laughed again. "What were you expecting an earl to do?"

"Yell. Demand a servant. Ignore me. Really, the fact that I was carrying an awkward crate shouldn't have even crossed your mind."

Brock's amusement faded. "Why not? You're a gently bred young woman working herself into an early grave."

"I am no such thing," she replied with heat. "Well, yes, I suppose I'm gentry. But I'm not working too hard. And you will never convince me otherwise. I am absolutely certain that the human form is remarkably designed to perform work of various sorts. As long as one does not do too much at first, you can do whatever you put your mind to. And it most definitely won't kill you."

"I'm sorry, miss, I meant you no offense."

She merely sniffed at him. "If you are quite finished resting, we could proceed to the ballroom. Or we could call a couple of footmen to finish the task. I would hate to do that, of course, because they are all busy elsewhere, but if you really cannot manage, there isn't much other choice."

"I can manage," Brock gritted out between his teeth.

"I could take one side of the crate," she offered cheerfully, moving closer as though she were going to grab hold of it.

He could smell roses and freshly baked scones as she neared him, and he again felt swept with a wave of weakness, but he managed to turn so the crate was no longer in her reach. Nudging her out of the way with his shoulder, he repeated, "I can manage." He didn't appreciate her smug smirk, but he ignored it along with the protests his shoulders were screaming at him.

"This is a really big house, isn't it?" he remarked to break the silence.

He was rewarded with her sweet laughter. "It most certainly feels like it when you're trying to accomplish something. Or when you are burdened in some way." She cast him a sideways glance. "You'll certainly think twice before you offer your assistance to the next damsel you come across, won't you?"

Brock grinned. "You're probably right, but I can be as stubborn as a goat as well, so it's doubtful that I'll be able to overcome my chivalrous side, even if this is a very good object lesson to think before leaping."

The girl returned his smile.

"You've never told me your name," he commented.

"We haven't been formally introduced," she replied, pursing her lips into a prim expression that did not sit comfortably on her pixyish face.

Brock wasn't sure how serious she was, but while she was correct, they had not been introduced, surely the informality of a house party allowed for conversing without an introduction. She had said the same thing the last time he had tried to ask her name. It was more rude, in his opinion, to not even be using her name. Not that he could actually use her given name, although he was sorely tempted, if he actually knew it.

While he was debating how to answer, her face split into a wide smile, and a giggle escaped her parted lips. "I was teasing you, my lord. You are far too serious, I am sorry to point out." She twirled around on the tips of her toes then swept him an elegant curtsy. "Do I really look like the sort that stands on ceremony?"

"Not at all," he agreed with her, his face likewise splitting into a grin. "But you are correct in that you should be more careful than you obviously are prone to be. Not everyone your aunt has invited has the best of intentions."

The girl's smile dimmed slightly. "I am always careful. And Aunt Violet wasn't the one who invited the gentlemen." There was a pause while she thought about it before adding, her tone confiding, "You could say she didn't even invite the ladies, except in an official capacity. Lester told her who, in particular, he wanted invited. Of course, Lady Violet and I used our own good judgment before following through on his requests. We weren't entirely confident that Lester's choices were the most sound."

Brock tried to contain his amusement, but he couldn't deny that he quite enjoyed the girl's humour. "But you still haven't told me your name," he reminded her.

His amusement deepened as colour flooded her cheeks. For all her responsibility around the house and her obvious hard work, she was still a young woman, unused to social interaction with men of the *ton*.

She again dipped into a curtsy, this one even more elegant than the last, he couldn't help but notice, admiring her fluidity and grace. "My apologies, my lord. My name is Lillian Susanna Shaw. Formerly of Sherton but now really of nowhere in particular."

"Shouldn't you be Miss Shaw of Ashburn Place?"

Her smile was wistful. "I can see why you might think so, but I'm really no relation to Lester. My aunt is his stepmother. Of course, she is the viscountess until he marries and makes her a dowager, but the viscount is no family of mine. So, I am here on sufferance. Lester would prefer me gone, but since I make myself useful, he hasn't forced the issue. But he will, if I'm not careful. Or if he gets too bored one of these days."

Brock watched as she looked away, apparently not able to meet his gaze, until it was obvious that an idea had occurred to her, and she turned back to him with a speculative gleam in her bright gaze. "Do you have many estates, my lord?"

Brock's eyebrows rose and so did the colour in her cheeks. "Yes, yes, I should know that already since you're the important Earl of Sedgwick, but I will admit that I have allowed my reading of Debrett's to lapse."

He could only laugh. He hadn't yet answered her question when she launched into further speech. "The reason I ask is I'm wondering if you might be in need of a steward or housekeeper on any of your estates. I'd be quite excellent at either position."

"If you do say so yourself," he couldn't help but mock, making her already blushing cheeks turn even more fiery.

"I apologize if that sounded immodest, but I have been informally trained in both positions and have enjoyed the work immensely. I, of course, wouldn't be able to acquire written recommendations from the lord or lady of this establishment, but the steward and housekeeper would certainly vouch for my abilities."

"Before you go any further, I'm going to have to interrupt you. I'm terribly sorry, but I couldn't employ a gently bred young woman in any of my households. It would be scandalous for one thing, and would make me highly uncomfortable for another."

Her face fell comically. "I suspected as much." Her sigh was dramatic but sounded sincere. "I guess it's companion for me then."

"I beg your pardon?"

"Lady Vi assured me the only position it would be acceptable for me to acquire is that of lady's companion. It is really what I'm doing now for her, but Lester refuses to pay me. And I cannot sit around for the next four years without making any extra money, besides the anxiety of never being certain if Lester would finally pitch me from the door."

"What is to happen in four years?"

"I will receive the Bequest and am going into business."

Brock wondered if he would ever hear anything not surprising issuing from this girl's mouth. "What sort of business?"

"A bakery. In my home village. It shall be quite spectacular. I'm quite good as a baker. I know, that still sounds immodest, but really, when one is trying to sell one's services, modesty is not the best virtue, wouldn't you agree?"

Brock had to laugh and agree. "I suppose you are correct, although I've never been in a position of needing to sell my services."

"No, of course, you haven't. You're a man, and an earl besides." Her glum tone made Brock struggle to keep his amusement in check.

"Wouldn't you rather marry instead of going into business?" He felt the frown forming on his face, but he wasn't sure if it was from puzzlement or if he was disturbed at the thought of her marrying.

The young woman shrugged. "That's what Aunt Vi is pressing for, but I'm not so sure that a member of the *haute ton* would really make me such a wonderful life companion. From what I've seen these last days with Lester and his friends, they do not represent well for the pack of you gentlemen. A sufficiently educated man NOT of the *haute ton* might be a possibility, but I haven't the first clue where I might find myself one of those," she added with a grin before continuing. "I would ever so much rather rely only on myself," she concluded, a shrug evident in her voice.

Brock was at a loss for words and was beginning to wish he had never begun the conversation with her.

Chapter Seven

L illian could have talked with the man all day. It was unusual that she was sharing so many personal details. And it even seemed so very natural. That fact scared the stuffing out of her. She had no desire to develop a *tendre* for one of Lester's friends. But really, how could the man be one of Lester's friends? The more she learned about him, the more suspicious he seemed. He was too watchful, too serious, too calm, too steady to be one of Lester's friends. And he was far too handsome for Lillian's peace of mind. She would like him gone from Ashburn Place. But the fact that he had written to his servants to send him more clothes left her thinking he wouldn't be vacating the premises any time too soon. She stifled her sigh. She would have to continue keeping an eye on him.

On the one hand, that wouldn't be such a hardship, she thought with a grin she tried to subdue when she saw his eyebrow quirk up in question of her sudden change of mood. But on the other, she didn't want to notice anything about the man. Not his lovely, quirky eyebrows, and certainly not the way intelligence shone in his gaze as he spoke with her.

"What is in this crate?" the earl finally asked in an aggrieved tone, causing Lillian to burst into laughter even as she felt hot colour splash up her cheeks.

"It's all the flatware that will be required for the ball tomorrow evening."

"And you were carrying it, why, might I ask?"

"Because I have all the spare footmen helping the groundsmen repair the damage to the side lawn from Lester's impromptu game of polo."

The earl blinked at her. "You really are the informal steward and housekeeper, aren't you?" He paused for a moment, gazing at her with puzzlement clearly displayed on his momentarily expressive features.

Lillian appreciated being able to read his thoughts, as he usually hid them so well. She couldn't help grinning at him, but she didn't bother replying.

"But why did the flatware need to be delivered to the ballroom?"

"So the maids can make sure it is in readiness. I certainly couldn't ask any of them to carry this crate."

"But you were carrying it."

"Well, yes, I could ask myself to do it."

The earl's laugh curled her toes and warmed her stomach. Lillian had to work hard to squelch the sensations.

"You are a strange woman, Miss Lillian Shaw."

Lillian just grinned at him. She couldn't argue with him. She supposed she was, especially when compared with the women the earl was probably used to interacting with. She wanted to be undismayed by his words, but she couldn't help being a little hurt by them. She tilted her chin up and refused to be shamed. Her feelings, though, must have been written on her face, as the earl quickly stumbled over an apology.

"I meant no offence, Miss Shaw. I only meant that you are very different than the usual wellborn women I have met."

"Do not worry about my feelings, my lord. I realize I am different. My parents assured me I am unique," she stated with a grin.

"I would agree with their assessment."

Lillian was surprised to see what appeared to be admiration lurking in his gaze, but she dismissed the thought. She doubted any aristocratic gentleman would admire her managing ways. Unless perhaps he had a bunch of motherless children. Then she might be considered a catch. The thought amused her. It mattered little. All she had to do was survive until she got her dowry from Sherton and she would be set. And this earl's handsome visage and intelligent gaze weren't going to distract her from her plans for her future.

By the time they made it to the ballroom, Lillian was relieved that she could dismiss the man but knew she couldn't be rude about it. If not for his help, she doubted she would have been able to manage the task. It had seemed like a reasonable idea when she had set forth from the cellars with the crate. It hadn't seemed so very heavy then. But she knew her arms and shoulders would be aching the next day, even though she had only carried it half the way. Surely the earl would be even more affected than she, as the nobility weren't prone to physical labour.

"Thank you ever so much, my lord. You saved me a great deal of effort."

She had to bite her lip to hide her amusement when the earl's cheekbones darkened with embarrassment. The man clearly didn't receive gratitude on a regular basis.

"It was nothing, miss. I'm sure any number of the gentlemen would have been happy to help you."

Lillian wasn't so sure. And Lester would have been furious if he had thought she was enlisting help from amongst his friends. "That's kind of you to say, my lord." Now she needed to be rid of him so she could get along with her duties. "Can I help you with anything? I know your own activities were interrupted by my plight."

"No, no, upon my honour as a gentleman, it was the least I could do. I'll just leave you to your activities, then."

Lillian was left blinking in his wake. He hadn't appeared to be in such a hurry to leave her company just seconds before. She wondered what had gotten into him. But then she shrugged and carried on with her duties. She had wanted to be rid of him. It was foolish to regret it when he arranged for it himself. She tried not to watch as he strode from the room.

Chapter Eight

L illian walked briskly into the library and came to an abrupt halt. Lord Sedgwick was trying to peer behind the bookshelf. She had thought he had been doing odd things over the past two weeks, but now she was certain. The man was snooping.

"Would you like me to summon a couple footmen to move the shelving for you? I must warn you, I fear it is attached to the wall, but they can help you determine that for certain."

She would have laughed at the comical expression on the man's face if she were not feeling overwhelmed with conflicting emotions. She had found herself becoming increasingly attracted to the man while simultaneously trying to avoid contact with him during the course of his stay at Ashburn Place. But now she was forced to accept that he was not the solid gentleman she had been starting to feel he was. He was a sneaky snoop, and she would now be forced to do something about it.

Lillian sighed. Really, what could she do about it? If she took the matter to Lester he would probably have her thrown from the house just on the principle of the matter. He would, of course, take offence if she were to accuse his friend of something so indefinable as snooping. And even if she could prove anything, she was so constantly on the edge of Lester's disapproval that it would take nothing more than her approaching him about *anything* to find herself suddenly homeless. But what could she do? Ignore the matter?

The earl broke into her thoughts with his stammering response. Colour stained his cheeks, but she could tell he was trying to brazen it out.

"I was admiring the workmanship of the woodwork in this room. I'll be having some rooms redone at Sedgwick and was trying to gather some ideas of what I would like done."

Lillian merely gazed at him, wondering if he truly expected her to believe him or if he was just counting on her polite behaviour to accept his words at their face value. She was surprised to see his colour heighten even more under her steady gaze.

"The steward might be able to tell you a little bit more about it, but I'm fairly certain all the woodwork in this room has been in place for more than two hundred years, so you won't be able to speak with the craftsmen." She allowed a beat to pass before she cast him a shrewd glance and added, "Not that I believe that is what you were doing. I feel compelled to tell you that I cannot allow you to snoop through Lester's belongings, my lord. This is not the first time I have found you looking through his rooms on your own. I think it might be time for you to find an excuse to be called urgently back to your estate. It shouldn't be that hard to think of something, since you are so recently inherited."

Before she could do more than blink, the earl had fairly flown across the room past her to the door, closing it with a soft but decisive click. Lillian hadn't thought the large man capable of such swift action. She also hadn't previously thought she ought to be nervous of him, but there was nothing foppish about him in that moment as he watched her with a serious, searching gaze. A frisson of awareness and trepidation made its way up her spine, and she had to fight to keep fear from displaying itself on her face.

"What is the meaning of this, my lord? It is hardly seemly for us to be behind a closed door. I would ask that you step back and allow me to pass."

"Not before you hear me out." He finally spoke, and it was in such a firm, determined voice, so very different from the jovial tones she had become used to hearing from him. Her heartbeat sped up even more, and this time it wasn't just from fear.

"I hardly think you are in a position to make demands of me, my lord."

Her fear deepened as his eyebrow rose and he looked down his nose at her. "Really, Miss Shaw? I think it is you who is hardly in a position to make demands or accusations of me, wouldn't you agree? You, yourself, have told me of your precarious position within this household. Do you truly expect me to fear you telling Lester whatever you might think you saw? Who is he going to believe?" Without even blinking, his tone returned to his usual one full of laughter. "Really, my dear, it is such a lovely bookcase, and I truly need to do something about the library at Sedgwick."

Lillian felt tears suddenly prickle at the back of her eyelids. Disappointment threatened to overwhelm her. Even though she had known she couldn't find one of Lester's friends appealing, she truly had felt drawn to the earl, despite their differing stations. Now she knew that not only was he not for her, he was even worse than Lester. While her aunt's stepson was a wastrel and a bully, he was open about it. One always knew where one stood with the viscount. But not so with the earl. He was a consummate actor. But which was the act? The fop or the intelligent snoop? And did it really matter? She needed to find a way out of the room, and then she needed to get away from Ashburn Place. She couldn't stand by and watch this man do whatever he was doing, but he was right, she couldn't go to Lester either.

Brock felt as though he had just kicked a puppy. The young woman in front of him had seemed so competent and unflinching in the two weeks that he'd been watching her; he was surprised to see tears forming in her eyes. But he couldn't allow her to compromise his mission here in Ashburn Place. The idea that crossed his mind caused his breath to hitch. Dare he take her into his confidence? He had never done so before, but he felt he could trust her, and he certainly found her to be intelligent enough to be of assistance. And with all her involvement at the estate, she might be in the best position to know where he ought to look. *But will her sense of familial duty cause her to refuse to help and compromise me further?* It was a risk he would have to take.

It felt that eons had passed while he thought the matter through, but Brock was fairly certain it had only been a moment, as she was still glaring at him with a mixture of defiance and fear mixed in with her hurt feelings over his words about Lester and her position at Ashburn Place. He was going to confide in her. It caused an unusual feeling in his midsection. A part of him was actually looking forward to sharing his secrets with her, but the rest of him felt slightly ill at the thought of it.

"Miss Shaw, I think you should sit down. I have something I need to discuss with you."

Brock was surprised by the defiant tilt of her chin. Despite the myriad emotions he had seen crossing her face, it would seem she was not prepared to receive his confessions with equanimity.

"I will remain standing, thank you, my lord. And I would appreciate it if you would allow me to leave this room. I may not have much standing in this household, but surely you must realize that I'm a gently born woman and as such, we should not be alone in this room."

"I have the utmost respect for you, Miss Shaw, and I apologize for detaining you. I will not do so for long, and I have no intention of compromising you in any way."

"Then allow me to leave."

"I cannot do that until I have secured your cooperation."

Brock was surprised to see amusement cross her features. "I am cooperating," she insisted. "I could, instead, be screaming."

With a sigh, Brock acknowledged that she was being as pliant as he could expect under the circumstances and began his tale. "I am here under false pretences," he began.

"You don't say," she replied, sarcasm loud in her tone.

Brock bit back a smile and continued. "The Home Office has reason to suspect that Shepley is involved in a plot against the crown, and I was sent here to find the evidence and information about the plot."

After a moment's pause, Lillian burst into gales of laughter while she began to walk around him. "You, my lord, are ridiculous. I don't know why you are snooping around, but you certainly came up with an entertaining Banbury tale. I'll give you points for your efforts. But I still think you need to leave."

Brock grabbed her arm as she tried to squeeze around him toward the door.

"I'm not telling you tales, Miss Shaw. I am breaking my vow of confidentiality in order to secure your cooperation."

"You cannot seriously expect me to believe that Lord Shepley is involved in some sort of plot against the king or Prince Regent. For one thing, I don't think he could be capable of plotting anything. For another, he counts himself a proud subject of the crown. He would have no reason to turn traitor to it. From what Lady Violet has told me, he actually wanted to go fight in the war. He is surprisingly patriotic. You chose the wrong story to tell me, my lord."

Brock blinked at her, forcing himself to resist the urge to pull her into his arms. Now was most definitely not the time to develop amorous intentions.

"It might not seem likely, but I've seen the evidence they have to suspect him. It is solid. But we need more information."

A huff of surprise passed her lips. "You're really serious, aren't you? You really believe Lester might be involved in some sort of plot? And you are here trying to gather more information? And now, what? Now, you expect me to help you because I've caught you?"

Brock had been right; the woman was astute. He waited to see how she would carry out the thought.

Pulling her arm from his grasp, she paced away from him. "This is ridiculous. Your evidence must be a mistake of some sort."

"I am surprised by your sudden loyalty to the viscount. He doesn't deserve it."

She spun around to face him. "I am not being loyal to Shepley. I'm being logical."

Brock continued to stare at her, keeping a close eye to ensure she wouldn't storm away from him or alert others to his intentions. He found her fascinating but needed to contain the situation. His silence seemed to spur her to further speech.

Lillian huffed an impatient breath. "Think about this, my lord. You've spent considerable time in Lester's presence over the past two weeks and presumably previously, in order to have been invited to Ashburn Place. Do you truly think him *inclined* to conspire against the crown, let alone able?"

Brock felt his resolve weaken, and he blinked over her words. Her face split into a smile, as she felt she was making headway in her argument.

"I can tell you, he's not all that bright. And he's the laziest man I've met. Not that I've met many, mind you, and all his friends seem to be similar, which leads me to think that you are gravely mistaken and wasting your time. If there truly is some sort of plot and you have been entrusted with some of the investigation, you would be better served to find someone else to investigate. Lester cannot be involved."

Brock felt his own lips turning up into a reluctant smile at her logic. He couldn't really fault her. Lester was dimwitted and lazy. But the evidence had been irrefutable. The dim viscount was involved. And Brock needed to know more about the plot.

"I see your point, but that doesn't mean you're right. There is proof."

"Can you show me this proof?" The beautiful young woman was still defiant. And still distracting. Brock wished he didn't need her help.

"I don't have it with me."

"So, you expect me to trust you on face value alone, my lord?" She sounded incredulous. "Because I have to tell you, at face value, there's little reason for me to trust you."

He opened his mouth to defend himself, and she interrupted.

"Don't bother saying I ought to trust you since you're a gentleman. Presumably, Shepley is supposed to be a gentleman, too, and I have my own reasons to distrust him, in addition to the fact that you're trying to tell me he's a traitor. So clearly, being a gentleman is no basis for trust."

Brock couldn't contain his amusement over her obvious disdain. Her ire only seemed to rise over his laughter.

"You find me funny now?" she sputtered.

He tried to sober. "It's not you that's funny. Your words were amusing. And this situation is beginning to feel out of my control, so my laughter might have been tinged with hysteria. I apologize, Miss Shaw."

Brock was surprised when her face split into a grin. The girl clearly did not hold a grudge. His admiration for her grew, but he needed to ignore the sensation.

"Thank you for your apology. It speaks well of you. It's rare for a man to offer a sincere sounding apology. But then again, you do seem to be an excellent actor."

Brock blinked again, narrowing his eyes at her. Was she being sincere? What a strange minx she was.

"This is not getting us anywhere, Miss Shaw. It is neither here nor there if being a gentleman translates into being trustworthy. You must trust me, as we don't have a choice in the matter, much as I am forced to trust you."

"But the difference being that I have never tried to appear to be anything other than I am."

"Now who's being facetious?"

Colour flooded her cheeks, and she tilted her head in inquiry. "Whatever do you mean?"

"You act as though you are the most skilled servant in Ashburn Place, but really you ought to be one of its daughters, debuting amongst Society, not serving it. Surely you are playing a role just as much as any I might have done."

The girl stared at him, struck silent by his words momentarily. She blinked in silence, mulling over his words, but then suddenly she was again grinning at him.

"Have you considered that someone might be duping Lester into being involved?"

Brock had to take a breath to keep up with her return to the original subject. It was as though she had suddenly accepted his reasoning that they were both playing roles and needed to work together. Or she was still trying to defend her aunt's stepson. Either way, the girl had a valid point.

"I had thought of that but haven't yet been able to find any evidence of anything aside from what I have already seen before coming here. And that, unfortunately, only implicates Lester, no one else."

"What form does your evidence take? If it's so irrefutable, it must be tangible. Is it a letter? Did he write a letter to someone telling them about some sort of plot? What could be such strong evidence that you cannot be convinced, despite how dull witted Shepley is, that he cannot possibly be involved in your conspiracy?"

"Yes," he answered reluctantly. "He wrote a letter."

"And you've read it?"

"Yes."

"Has anyone been able to verify that it is in actuality the viscount's handwriting? I've read there are experts in such things, although I find it hard to believe."

"There are experts, you are correct, although it isn't too terribly difficult to forge someone's hand."

The girl laughed. "You aren't really supporting your argument well."

"I'm trying to be honest with you."

"Very well, so you trust that this letter you have read truly is a work of Lester's hand. And in it he implicates himself for being involved in treasonous acts. What has he done?"

"As far as we can tell, he hasn't done anything yet. Although being involved in the plot is enough to be charged with treason," Brock added. "But we want to stop the event completely. They are planning an attack on the prince."

Brock stifled his feelings of attraction as the girl watched him; her intelligent eyes widened slightly and blinked rapidly as she absorbed his words. "Someone is planning to kill the prince? But why?"

"I would expect to disrupt the government and throw it into chaos."

"But why not the king?"

Brock was impressed with her reasoning ability. "For one thing, the king is in failing health. These conspirators must be thinking of a long-term effect. For another, there was already an attempt on the king. He is more heavily guarded now. And of course, with his poor health, he doesn't go out very much. The prince is far more active in his stead these days. He is a much easier target."

Lillian was nodding as though in agreement with his words. "And from what I've read, the prince isn't of a mind to listen to council, so he is likely to turn up periodically without any protection at all. I would say he's a vulnerable target if someone actually has it in mind to do him harm." She paused in thought for a moment. "But he seems to be such a sweet gentleman, I find it difficult to believe anyone would want to cause him any harm."

"You mustn't consider that it's anything personal. These villains just want to stir up trouble."

"But why?" the young woman insisted. "Trouble just for the sake of trouble? That seems too risky, doesn't it? Trouble for the sake of trouble is setting fire to your granny's shed, not trying to kill a prince of the realm."

Brock grinned at the imagery she conjured. And she wasn't wrong. "It's not just for the sake of causing trouble. When we know more, we'll understand the motivation. It is likely that another government is involved. If the kingdom is thrown into chaos with the death of either the king or the prince, we would be much easier to invade, wouldn't you imagine?"

Her gasp was sufficiently satisfying to bring a grin to Brock's face. She understood the seriousness of the matter now. Or perhaps not. She began to shake her head once more.

"There is no way Lord Shepley would be involved in a plot that would include an invasion of the kingdom. As I told you, he is loyal to the crown. He considers it his obligation as viscount."

"I will grant you that it is likely he doesn't realize what he is involved with. That doesn't make it any less dangerous."

Now she was nodding, her intelligent gaze locked on his. "No, in fact, it makes it all the more dangerous. If any of the participants do not realize the seriousness, they will not be on guard." She paused, looking away. "Very well, my lord, I will do what I can to help. I, too, am a loyal subject and cannot risk there truly being a plot against either of those dear men. Where all have you already looked? And what exactly are we looking for?"

Chapter Nine

Lillian tried to keep her focus on the task at hand – helping her aunt plan the table setting for the final meal of the house party. It was a struggle, though, because she was torn between relief that the party was nearly over and disappointment that she would no longer be seeing the earl. They had been spending more time together, endeavouring to discretely search Ashburn Place for clues as to Lester's involvement in the conspiracy. They hadn't yet found anything. Lillian was certain Sedgwick was wrong in his allegations, but they still hadn't searched the steward's office, so she had agreed to withhold final judgment until they had managed to do so.

"You aren't attending to a single word I've said, are you?"

Lillian jumped, and guilty heat flooded her cheeks. She offered her aunt a rueful smile as she put her arm around her in a sideways hug. "I'm so sorry, Aunt Vi. You're quite correct, my mind was elsewhere."

"Wherever could it have been? I would almost think you had developed a *tendre* for someone with the way you are acting."

Lillian's face heated even more. She tried to laugh away her aunt's words. "That is just ridiculous, Aunt Violet. There isn't anyone here that could possibly warrant my warmer feelings."

"Not even that handsome Earl of Sedgwick?"

Now Lillian's face was on fire, but she still tried to brazen it out. "Why would you ask that?"

"Because even I can tell he is a little out of place here with Lester's friends. Of all the men you've ever encountered, he seems most likely to be someone you would find interesting. And your lack of attention this morning tells me you have found *some*thing to interest you."

"I am amazed that you are able to keep your focus on the task sufficiently, to be honest, Aunt Violet. I saw your eyes straying toward Lord Avery far more often than was necessary this morning."

Lillian's embarrassment over her aunt's words wasn't enough to disguise her amusement when the viscountess' face flamed with her own discomfort.

"I was doing nothing so vulgar as to stare at the earl."

"Of course not, my dear aunt, you would never stoop to stare at a gentleman. But you were certainly glancing numerous times."

Lady Violet laughed. "Well you cannot blame me. The man is certainly attractive."

Lillian offered an answering grin. "That he is. That silver hair is surprisingly distinguished. I would have never thought I would consider an older man so handsome."

"I think it's the fact that he seems so spry."

"And the fact that all that silver hair is so very abundant. And it contrasts so deliciously with his blue eyes."

"And the crinkles at the edges of his eyes when he smiles."

Lillian laughed again. "I haven't noticed those. I don't think he's been smiling at me nearly as much as he's been smiling at you."

"Oh no," Violet protested. "The man does not approve of me. He hasn't been smiling toward me at all."

"I beg to differ," Lillian argued. "Perhaps not about the disapproval. That cannot be helped while we're in the same household as Shepley, but I'm pretty sure he's been smiling at you ever since he arrived."

"But his daughter told me he hadn't wanted to allow her to come."

Lillian shrugged. "If you had a daughter, would you have wanted to allow her to come to Lester's house party?"

Violet opened her mouth as though to argue and then shut it with a snap. "Very well, you have a point." Her gaze turned shrewd as she looked at her niece. "If we will follow that reasoning, then, I ought to do all in my power to get you out of this house, shouldn't I?"

Lillian grinned at her aunt. "Find one of your friends who needs a companion, and I'll be out of here in a heartbeat."

"That is not what I meant, and you know it."

"Aunt Vi, you and I both know full well that your stepson is not going to sponsor me for a Season. And I'm not sure if I would even want one. My idea is much better."

"But I came up with a brilliant idea to get Lester to do just that."

Lillian just looked at the viscountess with raised eyebrows, and the other woman continued.

"If I tell Lester I would like to remarry, he will be eager to be rid of me, I'm sure. He'll then give us the necessary funds, as he will have to agree that I would need a companion."

"But you don't want to remarry," Lillian protested.

"It might not be so very bad," Violet answered and then blushed as Lillian's gaze turned shrewd.

"If it was the handsome silver-haired earl, do you mean?"

Lady Violet protested. "I am not setting my cap at the man, if that's what you're thinking. Besides, I'm not sure if I would be able to get past the thought that he didn't respect me."

"I can see that respect would be important, but you haven't really gotten to know the man at all. Perhaps he could develop a great deal of respect for you."

There was a momentary pause while the two women smiled at each other, but then Lillian marred the peaceful moment with a frown.

"Wait a minute, you're just considering this for my sake, aren't you?"

Violet made to protest, but Lillian overrode her.

"Aunt Violet, you are not responsible for me. You have to accept that. You did your best when I was young and had nowhere to go, but I'm a fully grown woman now and can fend for myself. I would hate it if you ended up in a miserable marriage for the rest of your days out of some misguided attempt to set me up with a comfortable life. I will be perfectly comfortable when I can come into my funds."

"Ten pounds," Violet scoffed. "That's next to nothing."

"Only to someone who has gotten used to spending ridiculous sums, but I haven't. I swear to you, I shall be perfectly fine with my ten pounds and my bakery. I'll be better than fine, in fact. It'll be perfect for me."

"But that's still four years away."

"Four years, three months, and twenty-seven days, but who's counting?" Lillian laughed. "But if you could help me to find a position, the time will fly by, and I'll have all the more funding set aside to help with my bakery when I actually inherit."

Violet sighed. "Very well, as I promised you, I will write to my friend once the house is empty."

Lillian shuffled her papers and returned to the task at hand. "Thank you. Now, would you like me to seat you in such a way that you can discretely watch the handsome earl throughout the meal?"

Violet cast her niece a wry glance. "No, I want you to sit me beside the Earl of Sedgwick, so I can discover what you find so very fascinating about that handsome man."

Lillian laughed. "I told you, I am not fascinated with him in the least."

Violet didn't even acknowledge her words. "I don't see you writing, my dear. How am I to give you a good recommendation if you don't do as I ask?"

Lillian laughed again. "Very well, very well, I'm writing as we speak."

The rest of the interlude passed in equally pleasant camaraderie. Before too many moments had ticked by on the clock they were as prepared as they were going to be for the final evening.

"You're absolutely certain the cook knows exactly what we want?" Violet fretted.

"Completely certain. And the kitchen is stocked to the ceiling with every possible supply. There will not be a shortage, I can assure you. We also have a few extra girls from the village coming in for the day to help with any last minute preparations and cleaning duties as well as to ensure that the footmen will all be free to circulate with trays."

"You've thought of everything," Violet remarked. "I do think you ought to consider being a countess. It is well within your skill set."

Lillian burst into laughter. "You are irrepressible, my lady. Also within my skill set is to run a small bakery in my home town."

"Do you really think the Countess of Sherton will be that eager to support your small business? Surely she will consider it strange that a gently born woman has gone into trade."

"You are worrying overmuch. I know I will require her patronage, but from what I remember of her, she is not a small-minded woman. She will not begrudge me my efforts and will not stand in my way."

"She may not stand in your way, but you will need the support of the biggest house in the area, will you not?"

Lillian didn't bother arguing, relieved that her aunt was finally speaking about it as an accepted fact. "Perhaps you could write to her for me, after you find me a position as companion."

Violet rolled her eyes and laughed but allowed the subject to drop, returning to the original subject at hand. "Have you finished with the seating arrangements? I think that's the last of the planning, isn't it?"

"That it is, my dearest aunt. And now we will have the house back to ourselves in just another two days."

"Won't it be lovely to have a little peace and quiet?"

"Absolutely," Lillian agreed with wholehearted enthusiasm, although she doubted they would have total peace unless Lester were to leave with some of his friends. "Have you heard from Lester as to what his plans are?"

"No, and I haven't asked. I'm hoping one of his friends needs help choosing a horse or something."

Lillian giggled. "No doubt one will." Getting to her feet, Lillian excused herself from her aunt's presence. "I ought to check on the maids and make sure all is progressing with their tasks. And it must be time for you to start your evening toilette."

"You ought to be joining us for at least these final entertainments."

"Do you think Shepley has changed his mind about me?" Lillian kept her tone even so that neither her irritation nor her disappointment would show.

"No, you're right, he hasn't said anything. But since we've invited all the surrounding gentry, surely you must be included."

"Well, if I was to attend, we would have to rework the entire seating arrangements, and that would just be too tedious. Never mind about me. I shall have my festivities when the house has returned to normal. It isn't likely to be to my liking, anyway."

With those words, Lillian made good her escape. She ran on light feet up to her room to pass a comb through her hair and splash cool water on her face. Her tasks were not nearly over. She would have to hover over the rest of the staff until the exalted guests had dined, played, and were settled for the night. She hadn't been exaggerating when she said it would be her turn for festivities once everyone was gone. She was nearly exhausted from the work of keeping such a large entertainment on track. Especially when so many of the aristocratic guests thought that everything should revolve around them.

Lillian rolled her eyes at the thought of some of the demands that had been made, especially by the ladies. The only thing that had saved her was that, as a viscountess, Lady Violet outranked most of the guests. Only a couple countesses were of higher rank, and they were all older and polite chaperones of some of the overbearing debutantes. Lillian shuddered to think what would have happened if Lester had invited any duchesses. Not that any of them would have accepted his invitation, but it would have been a trial to bear.

Chapter Ten

The evening was just about over. The dinner had been a success. There hadn't been any broken or spilled dishes, and many compliments had been extended to the cook. The musicians were playing what Lillian was almost certain was the last dance. Most of the older guests had already sought their beds. Only the youngest guests were still stepping lively.

Lillian's gaze was ensnared by the Earl of Sedgwick, as he motioned her toward the back stairs. She felt her face pale. He wanted to search the steward's office. It would be better to wait until all were abed, on the one hand. But if they were caught by some chance, it would be easier to brazen out if there were still some guests about. Being caught wasn't an option, anyway. If Lillian was to help the earl, they needed to remain undetected. Lillian was still convinced there had to be some mistake about Lester's involvement. If she helped the earl with this last search, he would have to agree with her and leave with the rest of the departing visitors.

Bracing herself and squaring her shoulders, Lillian marched off in the direction he had indicated. Now was, no doubt, the best possible time to take such a foolhardy risk.

"I didn't see you about at all today," the earl commented quietly as they made their way down the hallway.

"Were you looking for me?" Lillian asked, surprised by his words. "I wasn't hiding. There is a great deal of work involved in having this many people around."

"I'm sure it is, although you make it look easy."

Lillian had to stifle her laughter in order to not be heard. His admiring tone made her even more nervous than she had been. Now was not the time, she admonished herself.

"The steward's office is just behind the viscount's library, the next door on the left," she whispered.

"I doubt anyone is about. We don't really need to whisper."

"Do you care to see what sort of reaction we would get if someone happens upon us, my lord?" Lillian was surprised at how relaxed the earl seemed. "Are you not trying to keep your quest quiet?"

"Well, of course I'm trying to keep it quiet, but everyone is either still dancing or already fast asleep. We shall not be discovered."

"I am not so confident, my lord. We need to be quick."

"Miss Shaw, do not be anxious. All will be well."

Lillian almost ground her teeth together at the earl's words. They were not helping to allay her fears. If anything, his easygoing manner was making it worse for her, as it seemed he was not taking the very real risks seriously. But she lifted her chin and chose to ignore the handsome earl and her own misgivings. She opened the steward's door and stepped into the room ahead of Lord Sedgwick.

The candles they had been carrying cast eerie shadows on the walls before they settled down. Lillian quickly lit several more, brightening the room considerably. She didn't want it too bright, lest the light spill out from under the door, but it needed to be bright enough for them to see what they were doing.

They made quick work of choosing which side of the room they would each start searching. Lillian wasn't sure if she was even doing it right. She had no idea what they were looking for but didn't want to ask any more questions. As the earl had said, they would know it when they found it.

Lillian quickly became engrossed in her task. She hadn't been in the room since Wilbur's death. The steward was the least comfortable of all the residents with her work on Lady Violet's behalf. He wouldn't meet with her since her uncle's death, insisting that he only answered to the viscount. Lillian had never bothered to argue. She didn't need any more tasks assigned to her, anyway. And one of her greatest aims was to avoid any conflict with Lester.

Not that searching the steward's room was going to further her efforts in that regard, Lily thought sarcastically before bringing her mind back to the task at hand. Her attention was quickly snagged by the small pile of papers she had found tucked into what looked to be the current ledger. She stepped closer to the light just as she heard footsteps in the hallway outside the room.

The breath stilled in her chest, and Lillian froze with fear just as the door handle turned. Looking around frantically for a place to hide, her gaze collided with that of the earl. She saw that his eyes were filled with sympathy, but she couldn't grasp why until the steward stepped into the room with Lester hard on his heels.

"What is the meaning of this, Lillian?" Lester demanded, his tone hard and cool. "Are you trying to make off with my important papers?"

Lillian's gaze flickered toward the earl and was stunned to realize the man had disappeared. She blinked for a second before looking back into Lester's cold eyes. Without flinching, Lillian brought her chin up and refused to cower.

"Not at all, my lord, I was concerned about a discrepancy the cook had mentioned in one of the orders we received from the butcher and was hoping to find the receipt so that I could confirm if it was, in fact, a problem before I brought it to your attention."

She felt rather proud of herself for her quick thinking for a brief moment before the viscount sneered at her words. "It is not your place to be concerned about such matters, even if I believed this tall tale. Ralph was going to show me some concerns he had with one of the accounts, but I think we've found the source of the problem already, haven't we? It is you who has been pilfering from my accounts, isn't it? Don't bother arguing, Lily. Your being here is unacceptable. You have no business in my affairs. You are no longer welcome to be receiving of my charity."

Lillian felt her eyebrows rise. "Of what charity are you speaking, my lord? I have received nothing from you."

"I have never owed you a single thing, and yet I have allowed you to remain as a guest in my home."

Lillian didn't bother to argue with his definition of guest, merely looking him in the eye and awaiting his next words. It was obvious he wanted her to beg. She doubted it would do any good, even if she could have stomached doing such a thing.

"You will vacate these premises immediately."

The steward must have had at least an ounce of dignity in him. He made to protest.

Lester acknowledged the man's discomfort. "You are too soft, Ralph. Very well, Lillian. You may remain until daylight. Never let it be said I'm anything but merciful."

Lillian didn't even bother replying. She turned on her heel and left the room with as much dignity as she could muster. How was she going to explain this to her aunt? The fear hit her as she got closer to her small bed chamber. What she had been dreading ever since Lester inherited had finally happened. She had been banished from Ashburn Place. And she had nowhere to go.

The thought of throwing herself upon the charity of old family friends back in Sherton turned her stomach, but there was little other choice. She could, of course, demand that the Earl of Sedgwick do something about her situation, but really, that wouldn't help. It might only cause her to be further ruined. And what kind of a position to help her could the man be in, anyway? He hadn't been willing to hire her as housekeeper or steward; it was doubtful he would be able to help her find somewhere to go. Besides the fact that he had done nothing to help her in the moment of her ruination. Lillian mentally waved her hand in dismissal to the thoughts. She understood on one level that he couldn't give himself away, but on another, the one that thought they had somehow become friends, she was deeply hurt that he had stood silent while she had been dismissed like so much rubbish.

Aunt Violet wouldn't be able to send her to one of her friends now that she had been banished. Lillian castigated herself. She should have insisted that her aunt find her a position before it came to this. She just hadn't wanted to leave her only living relative. But now she would have to. And under a cloud. It wasn't going to be an enjoyable experience.

Squaring her shoulders, Lillian refused to give into the fear that was threatening to overwhelm her. What was done was done. Perhaps it would actually be for the best, Lillian tried to encourage herself. She had been stagnating here at Ashburn Place. Now she was going to be forced to adjust. It was entirely possible that something good would come of this turn of events. Lillian couldn't, in that moment, think what that good might be, but she was willing to concede that it was possible.

When she reached her room, Lillian pulled the satchel she had used to bring her few belongings to Ashburn Place out from under the bed and carefully placed those few belongings into it. She debated over what else to take. All the lovely gowns Uncle Wilbur had insisted on buying her were a little outdated and more suited to a young girl. Lillian had only given in and allowed her aunt to have one gown made for her since her uncle had died. It was lovely and suited her perfectly even though Lily had rarely had occasion to wear it. It would be a wrinkled mess if she put it in her satchel, but it might be to her benefit to bring it with her since, if she ever had an opportunity to present herself for a position, it wouldn't do to show up looking like a street urchin. Not that anyone would be willing to take her on as a companion now, she acknowledged with a sniff. A cloud would follow her. Her respectability would be questioned since she would no longer be coming from Ashburn Place.

Lillian shook her head. Being at Ashburn Place hadn't done much to help set her up, she reminded herself. She had always managed to land on her feet. She would do so once more. She would have to ensure the fear she was feeling motivated her, not overwhelmed her. With a decisive nod, Lily squeezed in the last of her belongings that would fit in the one bag. She couldn't burden herself with more as she would most likely have to walk, since she wouldn't have the funds to hire transportation.

Aunt Violet would want to provide her with money, Lillian was sure. But Lily was also sure that her aunt had spent all her pin money for that quarter. It was certain Lester wouldn't advance her any at this point, since he would know it was to be for Lillian's benefit. Not that she would have taken her aunt's money anyway, but it added to the quagmire of emotions that they were sure to be confronted with when Lillian had to say goodbye to her aunt.

Forcing herself to lie down even though she was certain she would be unable to sleep, Lillian tried to still her mind, but the questions continued to chase themselves around in her head. Who could she trust? Who would take her in? Where could she go? Bad things could happen to young women who didn't have the sense to keep themselves out of trouble.

Lillian realized in that moment that the strongest emotion she was feeling was anger. Anger with herself for giving in to the lure of helping the earl. She had succumbed to pride. The handsome man had appealed to her intelligence, and she had caved right in. She had wanted to feel superior to Lester. Which was ridiculous. Everyone was superior to Lester, she thought with a small smile. But she had wanted to impress the earl. And now she was teetering on the precipice of a great unknown.

Taking a deep breath, Lillian quelled the nerves that threatened to overwhelm her. She swung her feet over the edge of the bed and sat back up. She wasn't going to get any sleep tonight; lying there wasn't going to do her any good.

How dreadful would it be to leave without saying goodbye to Lady Violet? Her aunt would be hurt, but it might be better for both of them if she just wrote her a letter. Lillian didn't want to take a chance on her aunt getting into trouble with Lester on her account.

Lillian made quick work of getting herself dressed respectably and tidying her hair. Picking up her satchel and leaving her room as silently as she could, Lillian bit her lip in indecision. There was an escritoire in at least one of the salons. She would be undisturbed and could explain everything in a letter she would slip under her aunt's door. It would be a *fait accompli* before her aunt awoke. It would be better than a prolonged, emotional leave taking. And the least likely to embarrass her aunt with guests still in the house.

Indecision assailed Lily, though, as she sat down to write. What could she tell her aunt? She needed to provide her with a direction of some sort so her aunt could remain in touch with her. Watching the candle sputter on the edge of her table absorbed her attention as she tried to figure out what was best.

My dearest aunt,

Please do not get yourself into a taking, but Shepley finally threw me out of the house. He had agreed that I could wait until morning, but I was too restless to wait and have decided to get a head start since it is a bright, cloudless night.

I beg of you not to ring a peal over him. It will only worsen your situation and won't do any good. I promise you, I will be just fine.

Lillian had to stop to brush an errant tear from her cheek. Just writing her farewell was dreadful. She had made the right decision not to do it in person. But where was she going to tell her aunt she was going?

I am heading for Sherton. It is time I checked on things there, anyway. I will make contact with old friends and see if I can get an audience with the countess. Perhaps I can find a position there until I receive my bequest. It will be the best circumstances for everyone. I promise I will keep you updated on my progress. If I have to move on from Sherton, I will ensure you have my direction.

Please, don't worry about me. You know I am capable and the friends in Sherton will see to me. It has been lovely to be together these past few years, but it is time for me to seek my own destiny now. I will love you forever.

Yours,

Lillian

Waving the paper gently to dry the ink, Lillian blinked rapidly to dispel the threatening tears. Now that she had stated her plan, she felt energized and motivated. And surely it wasn't much further than ten or fifteen miles to Sherton. She could walk the entire way and save her few spare coins. Thus decided, she left her satchel in the parlour and made her way as quietly as possible above stairs to her aunt's bedroom door.

Lillian had a moment of indecision as she stood in front of the solid oak. She knew her aunt would be hurt that she hadn't waited until morning so she could say goodbye in person, but Lillian knew it would be all the more painful for both of them if she didn't leave now. And with Lester's guests still in the house, there was sure to be a scene if the viscount found her still present. Or Violet would feel obliged to defend her niece in front of her stepson, and Lillian's ruination would be ensured if she were forced to explain her presence in the steward's office.

No, it was better for all involved if she did it this way. Lillian squared her shoulders for at least the fifth time that night before bending down and slipping the folded piece of paper under the door. Violet's maid would find and deliver it when she brought the viscountess her morning chocolate.

Chapter Eleven

T rudging along the road with her satchel rubbing her hip, Lillian silently lamented how much she had packed. She tried to remind herself she would be grateful later that she had managed to bring as much as she had and would, in fact, be wishing for more. But the bag was feeling heavier and heavier as the time passed. Glancing toward the moon, Lillian was grateful for its presence but wished the shadows it cast weren't so very creepy. Surely it couldn't be too much longer before the sun would start to rise, she reassured herself.

She was grateful that she had crept back into the steward's office to examine a map. Lillian had hesitated to do so, but she had decided she couldn't be more banished than she was, so there was nothing really for her to risk by entering. And the knowledge she had gleaned had served her well at the last crossroads. She had just been able to make out the writing on the small sign in the weak light and was confident she was on the right road.

Wondering how Sedgwick was feeling after what had transpired kept her thoughts occupied during the lonely hours of her walk. Lillian hoped the earl would be able to find whatever he was looking for to stop the treacherous plot, if there truly was one. She still couldn't believe that Lester was involved, no matter how angry she was with him for her banishment. He just didn't have it in him as far as she was concerned. But Sedgwick had been quite convinced of Lester's guilt. And nothing she had said or done could dissuade him. And now, here she was in the wee hours of the morning walking home to Sherton in disgrace.

Shaking her head to dispel the negative thoughts, Lillian spent the rest of the dark hours planning her recipes for the first things she would bake when she finally had her bakery. Before she knew it, she could see light beginning to peek over the horizon. As the light increased, so did her optimism. With relief, she read the next road marker confirming she was halfway to her destination. Despite the dark and the small noises that had made her jump through the night, she had managed to walk six miles thus far. She would reach her destination before nightfall for sure.

Her steps felt lighter and she picked up her pace despite her hunger and the bag weighing her down. Lillian was glad she had also stopped off in the kitchen on her way out the door and had managed to collect a small sack of provisions. She stopped next to a small stream that ran beside the road to wash her hands and get a drink. Her ordeal no longer seemed so very dreadful now that the deepest darkness had passed.

Violet read her niece's letter three times, certain that she couldn't possibly be understanding the words correctly.

"Are you all right, my lady?" her maid asked as the noblewoman frowned down at the paper in her hand.

"I am not completely sure, to be honest with you," she answered. Hearing the worry in her own voice, Violet tried to paste a smile to her face. It wouldn't do to alert the household if what was said in this letter was true. "But I do need to speak with my stepson. Could you please go find out from his valet if he is stirring as yet and then come back here and help me get ready? I will finish my chocolate while you are gone and be ready for you."

"Would you like me to also ring for your niece?"

"No," Violet answered sharply before forcing another smile. "The poor dear has done so much to help me out, if she is still sleeping, we ought to let her rest." Violet knew she wouldn't be able to hide anything from the servants for long, but she needed to know where she stood before she let anyone know, if she could help it. She hoped she might be able to get her niece back before anyone was any the wiser. Surely there couldn't be too very many routes to Sherton from Ashburn Place. A couple of footmen sent out in any possible direction should be able to collect her in no time, Violet assured herself as she sipped her morning drink. It did not satisfy her as it usually did. Her stomach churned in a way it hadn't done since she had met her dear, late husband.

It felt as though she had always been consumed with worry, even as a child. She had been far more aware of their precarious financial circumstances than had her brother, or so she had thought when they were children. As they had grown, her brother had confided in her that he had known and worried, too, but he had been in a different situation than had she. He had been able to do something about it. He had been hired by the town blacksmith as an apprentice and had actually been able to help with household expenses. Their parents had lamented his entering the trade but hadn't argued with the grouts he had been able to bring home.

Her marriage to the late viscount had allayed her anxieties for her future. But now she was back to those old feelings of uncertainty. *That dratted girl is far too independent for her own good*, the doting aunt thought with a shudder. Violet was torn between anger with the girl for running off on her own and pride in her for wanting to deal with her problems on her own. Violet could understand that sentiment. She would have never wanted to be a burden for anyone either. But her niece wasn't a burden. If anything, it was the viscountess who was a burden for the young girl, since she had allowed her to take on so many of her responsibilities. But the silly chit had taken it in her head that she didn't want to burden her aunt with her banishment. Violet could appreciate that as well, but she couldn't allow the girl to run off on her own. She would have to bestir herself more than she had in the last several years.

Realizing she had become habitually complacent, Violet determined to make a drastic change. She would have to ensure her niece was brought back, and she would have to procure new futures for both herself and her only living relation. She couldn't bear it if something were to happen to her brother's only child. Her stomach clenched at the very thought of the girl wandering empty lanes and roadways by herself in the dead of night. Even though she was a fiercely independent and capable young woman, she wouldn't be able to withstand an attack from wolves or bears or highwaymen.

Violet shook her head and swung her legs out of the bed. She would drive herself mad with her circling thoughts if she left herself here. What was taking her maid so long? Surely she should be back by now with word on whether or not her worthless stepson was out of bed. Violet put her cup down with a decisive clunk and bent over the washstand. The water wasn't warm, but she didn't have the patience to wait for new. And the cool water would brace her mind for the ordeal that the day would be. She would have to marshal her thoughts and see her way through whatever arrangements Lillian had left in place for the final day of the house party without letting on to the guests that anything was amiss. And she would have to make arrangements with Lester and rally a few friends to her aid.

She had to laugh. It would have been something she could easily manage before her husband's death had sent her into an emotional quagmire. But Lillian's help had allowed her time to heal. Now she had to return the favour for her darling niece. Violet would have to provide for the girl even if she didn't want it. Oh, she wouldn't force the girl into a marriage she didn't want, of course, but there was nothing to say she couldn't at least have a wee taste of a Season.

Feeling a little more restored to her equilibrium, Violet was ready to dress when her maid finally returned.

"I'm so sorry, my lady. It took me too long to ascertain whether or not his lordship was receiving. The viscount's man said he had been drinking until early this morning and doesn't expect him to be in any shape for an audience with you until just before the dinner hour."

"The dinner hour? But that's hours from now." That had not been what Violet was expecting, although now that she thought on it, she should have. Her reprobate of a stepson was such a disappointment. He had turned out to be nothing like his father. It was such a shame. Violet's late husband had been a dear, sweet man. But he hadn't kept a firm hand on his son, overcompensating for the boy's loss of his mother by being lenient when he should have provided more direction. And the stepmother hadn't been in any position to try to provide direction to the nearly grown man when she had joined the household. Her few attempts to provide a little direction had only caused friction in the household, so Violet had quickly learned to keep her thoughts about Lester to herself.

But now, what was she to do about her niece? She could probably still send out the footmen in search of her. The worst that could happen is that Lester would ring a peal over her, but the late viscount's Will had clearly stated that while she was in residence, she was mistress of Ashburn Place. So she was within her rights to send the servants on the errand.

"Please, let the butler know I wish to speak with him shortly. I will meet him in his office upon the hour."

Her maid cast her a puzzled look but merely dipped into a curtsy and said, "Very well, my lady. Do you wish me to do so before or after I dress your hair?"

"Could you send a footman from the hallway with the message right now and then we can get on with my toilette?"

"Very well, my lady."

Violet had to suppress a giggle. She hadn't been decisive about anything in over a year. It was little wonder the servant was unused to it. But the girl would have to adjust. Violet was determined to regain the control she had allowed to lapse in her grief. She realized that while she had wallowed, her heart had managed to mend, and she was ready to resume her life.

It hadn't felt that she would ever feel that way. Having Lillian around had been such a blessing. Violet was well aware that it was the dear girl's help that had provided her the needed breathing room to heal. But now the healing was done and life must carry on.

With barely restrained impatience Violet sat through the usually relaxing experience of having her hair dressed. The rhythmic sensation of the brush strokes would often almost send her to sleep, but now all she wanted to do was jump up from before the mirror and dash from the room. Inaction was driving her mad.

"Thank you, Margie, that will be all for now." She was finally able to dismiss the servant and leave the room. "I will be in the morning room until my appointment with Mr. Johnson. If I have need of you later, I will ring for you." The maid dipped a respectful curtsy and left the room. Violet took a deep breath before following her out.

She had at least fifteen minutes time to pass before she had arranged to meet with the butler. Violet supposed she could send for the man and have him meet her earlier than she had instructed, but she didn't want to draw undue attention to the situation. And the poor man had his duties to attend to as well. Many of the guests would be leaving that day, so he would be busy organizing the footmen to assist the departing guests.

The viscountess realized there wouldn't be many footmen to spare for her search for her niece, but she didn't much care. Surely there were enough for what she needed. And many of the guests had brought their own servants, so truly it shouldn't be that big of a bother for her to send a couple out to find

Lillian. She couldn't wait for days to hear from the girl. Now that she was thinking on it a bit more, it would be better to send groomsmen out after her, of course. They could ride quickly and find her before anyone would even note that she had been missing.

Why hadn't she awoken earlier? If she had realized Lillian was gone, she could have had her brought back before anyone was even stirring. But fretting about that now would serve no good. The circular thoughts were making her anxious. Violet glanced at the clock on the mantle as she stepped inside the breakfast room on her way by. There were still ten minutes before her appointment with the butler, but she was no longer willing to wait. She would go in search of him now.

"Good morning, my lady. You are looking well this morning."

Violet was surprised by the statement and the familiar voice that uttered it. Lord Avery. She felt her eyebrows rising up her forehead, but she dipped into a curtsy anyway.

"Good morning, my lord. Was your night restful?"

"Very, I thank you. I think it must have been all the dancing last evening, but I slept like a baby through the night."

Violet was unsure what to make of the earl being so friendly all of a sudden. It was most unusual, at least according to her brief experience with the man. Of course, he used to be friendly while her husband was still alive, but of late, it was clear his disapproval of Lester extended to her. It made for an awkward morning. She was about to dip into another curtsy and leave when he interrupted her in the act.

"Could I have a moment of your time, dear lady?"

Blinking back her surprise, Violet glanced toward the clock before answering the only thing politeness would allow.

"But of course, my lord, what can I do for you?"

"As you know, my daughter has made a little bit of a debut into Society. Her official debut will be this fall for the Season, but I have been allowing her to go about a little bit. She has been held back by multiple bouts of mourning and so isn't as young as some of the debutantes, but to me, seems far more innocent and inexperienced."

Violet merely nodded her head, unsure where the gentleman was going with his words.

"She strikes me as a lovely, young woman, my lord. You have done well with her."

The earl shook his head. "All the credit lies at the feet of my late wife. I was an unforgivably uninvolved father until my wife's death forced me to take a hand in the raising of my daughter. It is much easier with my sons. I haven't the least idea how to go on with the girl. A large part of me wants to lock her up in one of the towers at home and never let her out. But I have managed to convince myself that this is an unreasonable wish."

Violet smiled. "I am glad you have allowed reason to prevail." She tried not to glance back at the clock. It would be rude to leave before the man got to his point.

"I have observed you over the past day or two, and I am impressed with how you have managed to keep yourself separate from your stepson's infamy. And you have done a lovely job of organizing this gathering."

Violet stammered out a reply, still unsure what he wanted with her and uncomfortable accepting his compliments when so much of the work for the party had been arranged by Lillian.

"I was wondering if you might be comfortable escorting my daughter through the Season."

Violet blinked. This was not at all what she had been expecting.

"How could that be arranged, my lord? I am barely out myself."

"But surely your mourning has ended. You have been quite active during this gathering, and I can see that you are no longer wearing black."

"While it's true that more than a year has passed since I lost my dear husband, I haven't been active in Society. We weren't very involved with the Season even before he became ill. And surely you know that I never had a Season of my own. It was only by chance that I even met the viscount. And I'm fairly certain he only married me because he already had his heir. I am not high *ton*."

"Surely, my dear, you knew how much your husband loved you."

Violet felt heat rising in her cheeks. This was the most awkward conversation she had ever engaged in. And she really needed to be elsewhere.

"Of course, I know that. I merely meant I would not have been deemed an acceptable mate for him when he was young."

"I disagree, but that doesn't really matter at this point anyway. You are a viscountess. No one can dispute your acceptability now."

Violet stifled her sigh. "Of course not, but I am not an experienced matron of Society, my lord. If you are looking for someone to help guide your daughter, I am not the best candidate."

The earl's expression changed as though he were going to argue with her. Violet interrupted him before he could.

"I apologize, my lord, but there is something terribly important that I must take care of in a timely manner. Could we perhaps resume this conversation a little later?"

"We shall be leaving this afternoon."

"Of course, my lord. I do apologize. I merely need to confer with the butler on something. I could return in a few minutes."

"Very well."

Violet had to suppress her smile even though she was filled with anxiety over her niece. She felt as though she had been dismissed by the earl in her own home. It was ridiculous that she found even his arrogance attractive. But it had always been thus for her. A confident man was such an attractive creature. Perhaps it stemmed from the fact that her father had been such a weakling, which had lead to their precarious childhood. Her brother had not lacked confidence. Nor had her husband. She, on the other hand, could use a little of it herself. With a lift of her chin she hurried to her appointment with the butler.

Chapter Twelve

"But Walter, I have no intention of returning to Ashburn Place, and I don't understand why you are here."

"Her ladyship sent me. She says you are to come back right away."

"Walter, the viscount banished me. I am not welcome at Ashburn Place. Even if my aunt wishes it, that doesn't make it so. I am sorry that you have come all this way for nothing, but I cannot return with you."

"But Miss, I will get in deep trouble with the butler if I don't bring you back with me."

Lillian sighed, torn between her loyalties. She had made it to Sherton and was just about to approach the countess' estate when she had heard her name being called from behind her. She had never been so surprised as when she saw a groom from Ashburn riding toward her.

"I wouldn't want to cause trouble for you, Walter, but if I come back with you, I'll be the one facing terrible trouble."

"Her ladyship says there won't be no trouble."

"I am afraid she is mistaken."

The groom's eyes widened at her words, but a grin spread across his face. "That's not for me to say, Miss, but I need you to come with me."

"What do you intend to do if I refuse?"

Lillian couldn't help her smirk as the groom gazed at her in consternation. He could not force her to accompany him, and well he knew it. She almost felt sorry for him, but she wasn't about to give in to his demands just to make him happy. She also couldn't go back to the house party and cause a scene with Lester while his guests might still be there. That would be sure to put her beyond the pale if she wasn't already.

And then, of course, there was the fact that she was finally getting on with her plans for her future. Sure, this wasn't the way she had wanted to go about it, but she wasn't sorry that Lester's anger had forced her to get going. She hated leaving her aunt without saying goodbye and felt badly if she was leaving her in an awkward position, but Lillian was certain all the plans for finishing up the house party were in place, and the viscountess would be just fine. Once Lillian had made her arrangements, her aunt could even come and visit her here or wherever she would settle for the next couple of years. It would be best if she could find a position. All of this ran quickly through her mind as the groom stood and watched her anxiously, reminding Lillian that she needed to rid herself of the man. She wasn't returning to Ashburn Place, and her aunt would have to understand.

"Would it improve things if I wrote a letter to my aunt for you to take back with you? That way you could tell the butler you had done your best and that he ought to speak with her ladyship if he has a problem with it?"

"Oh, Miss, would you? That would be certain to keep me out of the fire."

Lillian grinned at his turn of phrase before sobering. She didn't have any paper. But they were in a town with an inn. Surely they would have some paper in their parlour. Of course,

Lillian wasn't planning to be a paying guest, but she hoped she would be able to arrange for the missive anyway. She marched toward the hostelry with the groom in tow, his horse bringing up the rear of their little procession. It would have been amusing if it weren't so very serious.

Wracking her brain as she went, Lillian wondered what sort of story she could tell the inn's host. She wasn't comfortable lying to anyone, but she didn't want to part with any of her few coins in order to gain access to the hotel. All she needed was a piece of paper. She didn't expect anyone to provide her with any food or drink for free.

"Good day, good sir," she greeted as she stepped into the entranceway and found the innkeeper hovering. Lillian was glad to see the groom was tying his horse to a post and standing nearby.

It was clear the host wasn't sure what to make of her, as his bow was brief and stiff.

"My aunt, Lady Violet Shepley, has been delayed, and I need to communicate with her. Would it be possible for me to send her a note to Ashburn Place by way of my groom?"

Lillian bit back a giggle as her words unlocked the man's hospitality. "Of course, my dear girl, come right this way. It isn't often we have anyone from Ashburn Place stop by in these parts. Your folks are most often heading east for the capital."

She was relieved that the man knew of Ashburn, but that Lester or his father wasn't a frequent guest. Otherwise he would have known that the viscountess' niece was not a member of High Society. The hotel, she was happy to note, appeared to be respectable and everything was clean. She didn't expect she would be extending her stay within its walls, but she wasn't uncomfortable to be there.

It did cross her mind that the innkeeper or his wife might be in need of more hired help, but now that she had associated herself with the Place, he would never consider hiring her. She bit her lip to bite back her groan of frustration. There was nothing to be gained from being upset. Lillian couldn't blame her aunt for being concerned about her and trying to look after her. She should have expected it. That dear lady was still trying to take care of her. It was hard for her to accept that her niece was a woman and not the little girl she had always known.

Seating herself at the small desk in the corner of the surprisingly well-lit parlour, Lillian quickly composed her letter.

My dearest aunt:

I appreciate your offer of help, but I am not able to return with the groom. Please make sure he doesn't get in trouble with Mr. Johnson. If you have any ideas or suggestions of a paid position for me, I'll be happy to hear from you, otherwise, I will be in touch with you when my plans are finalized.

Yours sincerely,

Lillian

Rereading it, Lillian hoped it didn't sound too cold, but she didn't want her aunt to think she wasn't firm in her decision. Lillian was not returning to Ashburn Place under any circumstances. She couldn't bear to live under the uncertainty any longer, not now that she had actually experienced Lester's ire. And she couldn't depend upon her aunt's charity. Uncle Wilbur hadn't provided sufficiently for her to be able to support them both in the style her aunt favoured. It was much better this way. If only she could convince the viscountess of that, she thought with a wry twist of her lips.

Lillian regained her feet as the innkeeper returned.

"I am going to bring you a pot of tea and some things my wife has just baked."

Lillian smiled. "It smells as though your wife is an excellent baker." She paused while the innkeeper preened. "Unfortunately, I cannot remain, but I thank you so much for your kind offer."

The man looked confused as she hurried from the room, but he didn't try to stop her, much to her relief. She had the note for her aunt and she hadn't had to spend any of her few coins to get it. While she was touched that the viscountess had gone to the effort of sending the servants to look for her, Lillian couldn't allow her aunt to disrupt her plans now that they were on the cusp of moving ahead. At least this way the groom would leave her alone and she could get on with things.

Speaking of the groom, he was waiting for her anxiously as she strode from the inn. He looked relieved as she waved the folded paper. Lillian could imagine the thought of trying to force her to accompany him had made him quite uncomfortable. Part of her felt bad for the man, but she couldn't allow that to dissuade her from her objective. At least, by writing the letter, she would hopefully keep the young man from getting into trouble.

Once she finally convinced the groom to leave her behind, Lillian set off for her old home. Not that she was going to disturb the new residents, but she was hoping her previous neighbour would be able to host her while she got herself situated. She didn't relish the thought of taking to the woods as her home, but since the weather was cooperating, she would do that if necessary. Whatever the case, she needed to find somewhere soon. Her sleepless night was starting to catch up to her.

Chapter Thirteen

B rock's conscience was biting at his stomach, but he ignored it as he took his leave of Ashburn Place.

"It was a pleasure, Shepley, even if the hunting wasn't all you had claimed it would be."

"I swear, it is usually much better. I think that foolish niece of my stepmother must have scared away the game because she thinks hunting for sport is cruel."

Brock laughed. He would believe the lovely young woman might have tried, but he expected she had her hands full with helping her aunt run the household. It was more likely the dissolute viscount had overhunted and not bothered to restock. And since the research he had been able to conduct had revealed that the steward of the large house was more crooked than a sword left out in the rain, he could be sure the man hadn't bothered to restock his master's fields.

It had taken every ounce of self control he possessed to remain silent as he stood behind the long curtains the night before, holding his breath so as to not be caught, and so he could hear what was said. The gentleman in him had nearly howled at the cowardly act of standing by while the young woman was mistreated, but the spy in him had forced himself to silence. *It is for the greater good*, had repeated itself in his head like a chant, which was the only thing that prevented him from stepping out and planting his fist into Lester's face. Now, standing in front of the dolt, it still took his full attention to maintain control of his temper.

"The chit doesn't know what sport is," was all the earl could say as his guilt reared up and cramped his stomach. He was the worst sort of cur for saying anything about the girl when he had done nothing to defend her while she was getting banished for helping him.

And she had helped him far more than she could possibly know. After Lester had packed her off and left with the steward, Brock had been able to take all the time he needed to search the steward's office. He wished he could tell the girl she had been right. Lester was a victim of the conspiracy. An unwitting accomplice. His only crime was being too stupid or lazy to oversee his steward. And too stupid to allow his stepmother's niece to oversee the steward either because Brock was certain Lillian would never have missed the obvious signs. But Shepley, no doubt goaded by his steward, wouldn't allow the young woman to be involved.

Nevertheless, Brock now had the evidence he needed and was anxious to be on his way to London to deliver his report to his overseer at the Home Office. From there he would go straight to his estate and never leave, if it could be helped. At least not until he had it well in hand. He realized as an earl he would need to provide the estate with an heir, but surely he could put that off a while longer.

The viscount was gazing at him expectantly, so Brock brought his attention back to the matter at hand. Trying not to allow his disgust of the other man to show at the last minute, Brock continued taking his leave.

"You must allow me to return the favour some time."

"Name the date, and I'll be there," Lester agreed promptly. Brock had to fight to prevent his eyes from rolling. It would be a cold day in Hades before he'd invite the lollard to his home.

"I'm sure we will be seeing each other about Town," was his answer.

"Will you be taking your seat in the fall?" the younger man asked eagerly. Brock would have thought the viscount's zeal for their friendship endearing, if not for his disgust with the other man's laziness and uselessness.

"I haven't decided about this year. There is still so much to see to on my estate, since I am so recently inherited."

"I know how that is," the viscount agreed. "We never got around to sharing stratagems for coping. Are you sure you can't stay a few more days?"

"Quite sure," Brock answered firmly but then tried to soften the blow of his words. "We'll commiserate over a fine bottle at White's when next we meet in Town."

"Very well." The viscount finally accepted his departure. "Safe travels. You never know who you might encounter on these wretched roads."

Brock merely nodded before making good his escape. He wished he could make straight for his horse, but he knew etiquette dictated he needed to take leave of the viscountess as well.

"You put on a beautiful party, my lady." Brock bowed over the older woman's hand gallantly, ignoring her girlish giggle.

"I didn't do all that much, but it was a pleasure to meet you, my lord. I must thank you for distracting my niece."

"I beg your pardon?" Brock was certain he must have misheard the woman.

"My niece. I'm certain you met her. Lillian Shaw. She is far too serious most of the time. It was good for her to be distracted by you."

"I didn't realize I had been a diversion."

Lady Violet dimpled at him. "Don't take offense, young man. You weren't meant to be, it was merely a happy happenstance."

Brock had to laugh over her words. "I still didn't realize I had been a diversion. Your niece doesn't strike me as the distractible sort."

A strange expression crossed the viscountess' face, but all she said was, "No, she doesn't, does she?"

"Is she around? I would like to take my leave of her before I go."

Another strange expression flitted across the woman's face before she smoothed it out into the perfect social smile. "I am sorry to disappoint you, but she isn't available at the moment. I'll be happy to pass along your best wishes."

"Thank you, my lady," was all he could say. There was no acceptable way for him to admit to the woman that he had been hiding behind the drapery as her niece was banished from the property. "My estate doesn't lie too far distant, but I ought to be going if I intend to arrive home before the sun sets."

"It was a pleasure to meet you, my lord. No doubt we will cross paths again before too very long."

"Do you intend to go up for the Season, my lady? I didn't think you had done so in the past."

"My late husband wasn't a big fan of the social scene, so we didn't spend very much of our time there. Then, too, I have been in mourning off and on, most notably for my viscount. But I do think a change of scenery would do me and my niece good."

"Oh, is she to accompany you?" Brock was surprised. He didn't think that would quite fit with the girl's bakery plans, but what did he know about the workings of the female mind?

"It will be highly diverting," was the lady's uninformative response, leaving Brock no further ahead.

"I will wish you *adieu*, then, my lady."

"Take care, my lord," the viscountess murmured as she dipped into a curtsy.

Brock felt the older woman's gaze on his back as he left the room, but he didn't bother to turn back around. He wasn't sure what would be revealed on his face, so it was best to just get on with his responsibilities. He regretted the collateral damage to the young woman, but the nation was at risk; there was nothing much he could do about her.

He made quick work of saddling up his horse and getting away. Relieved that London was about the same distance away as his own estate, it wouldn't tax him excessively to head in the "wrong" direction. He would far rather be heading home, but he was anxious to see this assignment to a close so he could get on with his life.

There was a degree of frustration as his supervisor was not available when he arrived at the Office. As a result, Brock had to make himself comfortable in his London townhouse for the night. His few staff members twittered about in distress over his unexpected arrival. It took a degree of effort to settle their ruffled feathers and assure them that he expected little from them as he had arrived unannounced. Thankfully, he kept a supply of appropriate clothing on hand and was able to kit himself out for an evening.

Despite most of Society having retired to their estates, there was always something going on in the Capital, and the earl was not disappointed. He finally found his quarry at the theatre.

"Sir, if I might have a moment of your time?"

"Sedgwick! What a pleasant surprise." The lack of sincerity was evident in his tone, but Brock managed to ignore it. "If you'll excuse us a brief moment? My friend is new to Society." The man excused to his friends as he gestured for Brock to precede him.

"I am sorry to interrupt your evening, sir, but I have information I thought you would need at the earliest moment."

"Surely it could have waited until morning, could it not?"

Brock shrugged. "Surely the nation's security shouldn't be left until morning, sir."

He stifled his amusement at the other man's ire. Brock outranked the man socially now that he had inherited, a fact that did not sit well with his social climbing supervisor. Brock wondered why it wasn't someone of higher status leading this investigation, but he well knew that aristocratic blood did not guarantee loyalty or intelligence. He didn't much care about status, but he knew the other man surely did. He wouldn't miss this scene one little bit. Thoughts of fields full of sheep and a dog at his heel kept him patiently awaiting the other man's return to his normal calm.

"Well, out with it man. You interrupted my intermission for a reason. What was so very urgent?"

"I found the evidence you were looking for. But it's not the viscount who is guilty. Well, his guilt lies in being a lazy oaf and not knowing what is going on under his very nose, but not treason. It is his steward who is making use of his position."

"That's nearly as bad. Being an accessory, even if you don't realize it, carries guilt."

"Perhaps, but it is going to be far less tricky to arrest a steward than a viscount, wouldn't you say, sir?"

"True, true, I can't argue with that," the man agreed grudgingly. "Do you have the evidence with you?"

"No, sir, I didn't think you would want to be responsible for it at the theatre. I could drop it off to your office first thing in the morning as I leave Town."

His overseer at the Home Office was a proud man who couldn't stand the fact that he had to, at times, rely on members of the *haute ton* for his intelligence work. He wanted to lord it over his underlings and hated to acknowledge Brock's position in Society. It had gotten worse ever since he had become the Earl of Sedgwick. While Brock had enjoyed his years of service, he would most certainly not miss this man.

"You could have done just that, then," the other man grumbled. "You needn't have interrupted my evening."

"My apologies, sir, I thought you would want to know at the earliest opportunity." Brock couldn't prevent the slight sneer in his voice. He had so little respect left for the man in front of him.

"Of course, of course. I suppose you've done just as you ought. Bring all that you have to the office at first light. There is another matter I would have you look into."

"No." Brock nearly ground his teeth as he restrained his tone but uttered the forceful word. "I was promised an honourable discharge once this last matter was concluded."

"Well it's not concluded yet, is it?"

"My part in it is. I've done as you asked for years. Now, I'm finished."

"Play time is over then, is it, my lord? You can't be bothered with helping your sovereign now that you have lands of your own to tend?"

Brock held himself still, containing his rage. "I've served you and the king faithfully and will continue to serve my sovereign's interests, just in a different capacity. But have you forgotten that you gave me your assurance in writing?"

The older man blinked at him; obviously he had forgotten. "Must've been in my cups when I did such a daft thing. Very well, Sedgwick," he admitted grudgingly. "You have done your duty well, as you said, for many years. You will be missed. I trust we can call on you if we ever are in dire need."

Brock bowed, not promising anything but also not ready to cut all possible ties.

The next morning, as soon as the sun was peeking over the rooftops, Brock presented himself in the small, nondescript building where he always received his assignments. Despite his eagerness to enjoy the quiet life of a country gentleman, he knew there would be times he would miss this work. A small part of him was grateful that his overseer wasn't cutting all ties with him. Perhaps he would regret that later, or there was a slim chance he would wish to return at some point. As the man growled out for him to enter his office, Brock acknowledged with a wry twist of his lips that the chance was very slim indeed.

After he handed over the few pieces of evidence he had and rehashed the matter thoroughly, Brock was finally excused. It felt to him as though he had been in the cramped offices for half the day, but he could tell by the light that it had probably been little more than an hour. He would easily make it to Sedgwick and his new life of freedom.

As he left the soot of London behind, his mind was torn between anticipation of all his plans for his estate and concern over Lillian. He was nearly certain that Shepley would have relented come morning. But he didn't really have any reason to be so confident. The viscount was a lout, after all. No gentleman would turn out a gently bred young woman into the streets like that for real, though, would they? Surely he had been bluffing. Brock shoved the disquieting thoughts to the back of his mind as he contemplated how to best increase the crop yields for the next planting season.

Chapter Fourteen

Violet was standing at the window rather absently staring out but not really seeing anything. She didn't imagine she would actually be able to see her niece coming back, but it made her feel as though she were doing *something* while she waited for the grooms and footmen to return. Surely one of them had found the girl by now.

She had finally spoken with her stepson, though it had been an uncomfortable interview. The young nobleman had already been in his cups. Or still was, Violet hadn't been completely clear on that. It would seem he was disappointed his friends were leaving him. He clearly wasn't in the proper frame of mind for the conversation she wished to have with him. Foolishly, she had pressed on anyway.

"I think it is time for me to leave off my mourning, Lester, and go up to Town."

"Really? It has barely been over a year."

"Would you say you are still in mourning, my lord? You barely put on an armband, and you certainly haven't left off your debauchery."

"Everyone grieves in a different way," he said, now sounding both churlish and defensive.

Realizing she needed to placate him rather than antagonize, Violet tried to alter her tone. "Of course, of course. And I will be grieving the loss of your dear father for the rest of my life.

But staying here with you at Ashburn Place is too lonely for me. Especially since you have made it clear that Lillian is no longer welcome."

"The girl was searching through my things," he protested. "A man cannot be expected to put up with that."

"What things was she searching through, my lord? I find it hard to believe she would do something so ill bred."

"I found her in the steward's office, going through his papers."

"Really? I'm surprised you were there at night," Violet mused before continuing. "Did she tell you why she was there or what she was looking for?"

"It didn't matter why. It wasn't her place to be meddling with anything. I sent her packing. She isn't to set foot on my property again."

Violet wanted to yell at the ungrateful man but made an effort to calm her tone. "I can understand your irritation, my lord, but the girl has been of remarkable help to me these past fourteen months. Since your father's death, I haven't been able to manage the household, and she took over everything for me. I think it is probably my fault if the girl overstepped. She has gotten into the habit of thinking it is her job to look after Ashburn Place, and I'm sure that's why she was in the steward's office."

Violet wasn't actually certain of that. She was fairly sure the girl had never stepped foot in there before, as the steward had made it quite clear he was not going to give up any of his responsibilities into her hands, unlike the viscountess and the housekeeper. But it seemed likely, knowing how managing her niece was. She was no doubt trying to be helpful. It seemed to be the girl's aim in life – to be useful. And she had been. Violet would like nothing better than to ensure that she continued to be. She just needed to get her back.

"What do you want, Violet? I'm starting to get a headache."

She actually almost smiled at his petulant tone but managed to restrain it. Violet had never been able to forge a relationship with her stepson. She had hoped that, in time, it would have happened. But the death of his father had put an end to any attempts at civility.

"Since you obviously don't want me here, even though your father's Will arranged for it, I think it time that I remarry."

The viscount blinked at her, obviously not expecting this and unused to her firm tone.

"Do you really want to replace my father so soon?"

"Of course not. Your father is irreplaceable. But I'm not in my dotage. And I want a home. This is no longer a home for me. Especially without Lillian. The servants do their best, but they aren't family. And you don't wish to be my family. I want a family of my own. I want a home." She trailed off, realizing how very true her words were. She wasn't just doing this to protect her niece. She *did* want a home of her own. Perhaps she really would remarry. Violet ignored the flash of Lord Avery's face that flitted across her mind. Now was most certainly not an appropriate time to think of him.

Firming her tone, she continued. "You will provide me the funds to make a splash during the next Season with my niece, Lillian, by my side."

"I will not provide for that girl."

"You will, if you don't want me on your hands for the rest of your life," Violet argued before reasoning with him. "Surely, you realize I cannot go to Town without a companion. She is the most reasonable choice. It isn't as though you have any sisters or cousins I could take with me."

Lester blinked at her as though he were confused by the conversation. "But the girl has left, hasn't she? I doubt she'll be accepted into Society anyway. All the guests here have seen here as a servant."

"No one here even noticed her in that case. Do you really think any of your friends take notice of the servants?"

"They do when servants look like her," he mumbled.

"Well then, you will have to present her," Violet declared.

"Have you run mad? I've never presented anyone, and I'm certainly not going to present your managing, mealy faced niece."

"My niece is a beautiful young woman who has had to be strong for her circumstances. She is neither mealy faced nor managing." At his sarcastic expression, Violet amended her statement. "All right, maybe she is a little bit managing, but it's only because her circumstances have made her so. If you sponsor a Season for her and present her, you will have her off your hands for good. And me, too."

"I already have her off my hands. And I don't mind having someone around to run my household, so I don't need you off my hands." The infuriating young man offered her a satisfied grin at that and took another swig from his tankard.

"Perhaps we should discuss this later," Violet finally said through her strained lips, every effort required to hold onto her temper. Without another word, she turned on her heel.

Now she was standing at the window hoping her niece would return but still no further ahead in providing for the girl. Violet sighed. Maybe she really ought to do as Lillian had asked and find her a position as companion to one of her older friends. Violet recalled her promise to write to her friend about it. That might help pass the time. But that was surely not the best future for Lily, her heart protested.

There was the sound of someone clearing their throat at the doorway, causing Violet to startle and whirl toward the noise. With her hand clutched at her throat, she was surprised to see Lord Avery at the door.

"Good afternoon, my lord. Are you and your daughter leaving now?" She hoped she didn't sound too eager for their departure, but Violet was no closer to feeling comfortable in front of the handsome older gentleman.

"Yes, my lady, but I was hoping you and I could speak for a few minutes before we do."

Violet knew her smile couldn't possibly reach her eyes, but she pinned it to her lips anyway. "Of course, my lord, should I ring for some tea?"

It truly was unfair how appealing the man was, even though he was aging. *Why can't women have that same blessing*, she wondered as she stared in a daze as his smile spread across his face, reaching all the way to the crinkles in the corners of his eyes. She really liked how his eyes lit up when he grinned like that. She knew an answering smile was beginning to stretch her own cheeks.

"There's no need to disturb your housekeeper. If I understand correctly, she injured her leg?"

Violet blinked up at him. "Have you set spies into my household, my lord?"

Much to her surprise, pink tinged his cheekbones as he bashfully answered. "In a manner of speaking, I have, I'm sorry to say."

"Whatever for?"

"I wanted to discern if you would be an appropriate addition to my household."

"I beg your pardon?"

"I was hoping you would consider the possibility of joining my household."

"I heard your words the first time, my lord. I think you need to explain their meaning, not repeat them." She could hear the dry sarcasm in her tone, but didn't much care. What could he possibly be thinking?

The earl cleared his throat again. "I could use a new countess, my lady."

"You could, could you? And what does that have to do with me?" While Violet felt a little flutter in her midsection at his obvious meaning, she had no intention of aligning herself with a gentleman who could not even declare himself properly.

"I am making a mull of this, aren't I?"

"It would seem so, my lord." Violet softened her words with a smile, since it seemed he wasn't trying to demand her presence in his home.

"The thing is, my lady," he began before interrupting himself. "Actually, might I have your permission to address you by your given name? This hardly seems the type of conversation one ought to have with formality."

Violet giggled. "Very well, my lord, you may call me Violet, if you'd like."

"And I would very much like it if you would call me Leopold, or Leo."

"That might take some getting used to," she replied, feeling shy all of a sudden.

"You can practice," he answered softly, his warm smile returning. "As I was saying, Violet, the thing is, I have known you for quite some time."

"You haven't really known me, my lord, I mean Leopold. I was your friend's wife, and I was friends with your wife, at least briefly."

"That's true, but my dear wife thought very highly of you those few times you met. And I know Wilbur's life changed for the better when he married you. I've known him since we were boys. He was never so happy as he was the few years he had with you."

"I thank you for saying so, my lord, but what does that have to do with now?"

"It's Leo," he reminded her. "And I'm trying to get to that. As I mentioned earlier, my daughter is about to make her debut. She will be gone from my household soon. That is as it should be, of course. My two older children have already married. I will soon be completely alone. I don't want to be alone, and I don't want my children concerning themselves with me. I want a companion to carry on with life. I don't think I'm anywhere near cocking up my toes. There is still much of life I intend to enjoy, even with my children gone. But I don't want to do it alone."

"Are you trying to say you want me to come live with you so you aren't alone?"

"Yes, that's exactly right."

"In what capacity, my lord?" Violet could hear the offence clearly ringing in her tone of voice. He had said he needed a new countess, but surely he hadn't meant her. Was the man looking to hire her as a housekeeper? Or was he offering her a completely disrespectful position?

"As my wife, of course."

Violet sat back and blinked at him. She didn't much care if she looked like an owl. She knew her eyes were probably as wide as saucers. While she had been telling Lester she would like to find a new husband, she hadn't truly thought she would. But here she was, without even the bother of a Season, receiving an offer. True, it was the least romantic offer she had ever heard of, but it was an offer nonetheless.

"This is rather sudden, isn't it, Leo? And were you not, just a few days ago, telling me that I was questionable association for your daughter?"

Colour once again tinged the earl's cheekbones, and he had the good grace to look sheepish. "It isn't so very sudden. I thought you were desirable even when you were married to my friend, much to my shame. But I fought those thoughts and feelings. I fought them for a long time. And it wasn't you who is bad association, it is your stepson."

"Would you expect me to cut him from my life?"

"Not necessarily, but I haven't seen any evidence that you are particularly close with him."

Violet finally allowed herself to relax from how horrified she was. She had to smile over his words. "Well, we aren't close. He was terribly resentful of his father remarrying. Which actually makes me hesitate over your suggestion. I have had the experience of disapproving stepchildren. I am not certain I would wish to repeat the experience."

"Do you think you'll find a single man without a family to marry?"

"Who says I must remarry?"

The earl looked embarrassed once more. "I have made a complete hash of this, haven't I?"

Violet smiled. "Maybe a little."

"I was hoping you would fall in with my plans, and we could just carry on comfortably. That isn't going to happen, is it?"

"Probably not."

"Do you truly wish to remain here at Ashburn Place as a grieving widow?"

"Not necessarily."

"Would you allow me to court you, then?"

Violet's heart soared at his words. "Would you really court me?" She knew her eyes were probably huge in her face once more but for a far better reason.

"It would be a pleasure, my dear Violet. But I must warn you, I am not particularly patient."

"Nor am I, to be honest, Leopold. And neither of us is getting any younger. But this is a rather large decision, and I don't wish to enter into it lightly."

"I don't really want to wait until the next Season. That's months away."

Violet chewed on her lip and glanced toward the window once more. The earl was no simpleton.

"There are other things weighing on your mind, aren't there, my dear? Do they impact your decision?"

"They do, as a matter of fact. Did you know I have a niece?"

"I believe I met her while visiting with your husband in the past. I didn't see her while we've been here, so I assumed she had married and we just hadn't heard about it."

Violet sighed. "No, she is still here. Or rather, she was up until last night. Lester hasn't been happy about her being here, as she is no relation of his. He kicked her out last night and she walked away in the middle of the night, merely leaving me a note."

"Is the girl daft?"

Violet smiled. "Not in the least. But she has the most outrageous independent streak. She didn't want to cause a scene with the house full of guests. And she didn't want to make trouble for me with Lester. And if I know her at all, she probably couldn't sleep, so she decided not to wait until morning to leave."

"We can take her in," the earl assured her. "Or rather, I could have my married daughter take her in, as I'm not sure I want such an independent creature influencing my impressionable younger one."

"While I can't blame you for feeling that way from the little you've heard, she really is a darling girl and I'm sure would influence your daughter for the good. She is a steady, hard working girl. I wouldn't have been able to keep the household together since Wilbur died without her. It is my dependence upon her that caused her to be so very independent. She had no one else, you see. Her parents died a few years ago. That's when she came to us. Wilbur had every intention of taking her up to London for a Season, but then he died and he hadn't made any arrangements for her. And my portion isn't enough to provide a Season for her. The viscount never expected to die any time soon."

"Very well, I can see what you're saying. But do you know where she is?"

Violet bit her lip and looked back toward the window and shook her head. "I've sent out some grooms to search for her. I should surely be hearing something soon."

"But you're worried and cannot be bothered with my little problem right now."

His kind tone actually brought tears to Violet's eyes.

"Loneliness is not a small problem, Leopold, and well you know it. But I deeply appreciate your understanding."

"When you get your niece back, would you and she be willing to come to Orchardside for an extended visit? I could have all my children come so you could meet each other. Then you could decide if you would consider taking on stepchildren and a widower."

Violet glanced back toward the window and bit her lip. He didn't realize what a huge thing he was asking.

"Might I ask you a question, my lord?"

"Only if you preface it with Leo or Leopold." It was a reprimand but said with an attractive smile that made Violet's heart rate increase and heat rise to her cheeks.

"Why me? You're a handsome, seemingly healthy, clearly wealthy nobleman. Surely, you could have your pick of any widow and even of the debutantes, if you were of the mind for it."

The earl interrupted. "No, please, I beg of you. I will only be able to handle one more debutante and that will be to marry her off to someone else, not take on that responsibility myself."

Violet laughed. "Very well, no debutantes, but I'm not the prettiest, nor the wittiest widow around, and I don't even have a good track record of running the household. My niece has been running things since Wilbur died. So again, I ask you, why me?"

Leopold laughed. "Why did you marry Lord Shepley? You had maintained your unwed state much longer than was the norm. There must have been something about him that made you take the risk."

Violet nodded but didn't speak.

"There's just something about you. I could argue that you *are* the prettiest widow. In my eyes, you could rival even the veriest diamond of the first waters that made her curtsy during the Season. But it's all that makes you you. I didn't think I would find it again. I haven't been in a hurry to remarry. I could have done so right away in order to have help with the raising of my youngest. But I didn't want to even consider it right at first. And then, not just anyone would do. And I think you'll do quite nicely."

Violet's heart soared. It was the perfect thing to say. It might not have been the most eloquent words she had ever heard. The novels she read from the circulating library would surely scoff at the lack of passion in his words. But she would have been intimidated if he had made a fierce declaration of unending passion. This she could work with. If she ever smoothed things out with Lillian, anyway.

"My niece and I would be delighted to spend some time on your estate this summer, my lord... Leo," she stammered with a smile.

"Wonderful," he answered, clasping her hand. "Would you like my daughter and me to stay another day while you figure things out with your niece?"

Violet tightened her grip on his hand and gazed at him in indecision. "I'm not sure. A part of me would prefer that no one was here when she returns, so there is no risk of a scandal attaching to her. But what if she doesn't return? Lester will be of no use to me. I am certain he will raise no hue over her absence, as it is entirely his fault that she isn't here." She paused for a moment, glancing once more toward the window, not wanting to meet his gaze. "Actually, the fault lies with me as well. She has been asking me for weeks to help her find a position as governess or companion, but I haven't wanted to part with her."

"Why would the girl want a position? Are you quite certain she is all right in the head?"

Violet laughed but nodded vigorously. "Quite certain. You see, she intends to open a bakery. The town she grew up in has a dowry for the impoverished young women of the town. A bequest from an old bachelor. There is some sort of story in his past, but I don't know the details. Anyway, Lillian is to receive this bequest in a couple years, if she remains single. She would receive it upon her marriage or when she turns twenty-five if she doesn't marry. She intends to take those ten pounds and open a bakery. But she would rather earn a little more in the meantime. Being here with me was not a paid position for the girl. Lester refused to pay her, and she wouldn't accept any money from me apart from a little pin money, and even that I had to force upon her."

"I suppose she sounds like a sensible girl." His tone was grudging but beginning to fill with respect. "Why didn't you wish to help her get a position?"

"Because she's a lovely girl both inside and out and ought to be married, not slaving away to support herself."

The earl gazed at her steadily, causing Violet to squirm. "You're still waiting for me to say whether or not I wish for you and Katherine to remain here with me, aren't you? Very well, yes, if you would, that would be lovely. I could use the support. Thank you. But are you certain your daughter won't mind?"

"She will probably giggle and ask if she can go riding with Lester."

Violet winced over his words. "Oh dear, perhaps you ought to leave then."

Leopold laughed. "Not at all. The good news is, I don't think Lester has any interest in getting himself leg shackled any time soon. From what I can ascertain of him, while he's a wastrel, he isn't intent on compromising any wellborn young women."

Violet was divided in her feelings on the earl's assessment. She wasn't impressed with her stepson at the moment, but she had to agree. Except that Lillian was a wellborn young woman that he very much had compromised by putting her out of the house. Glancing once more toward the window, she rose to her feet.

"If you'll excuse me for a few minutes, I have to confer with the butler." She paused. "And I suppose I ought to speak with the housekeeper to mention that you'll be staying with us another day. Lillian would normally handle such matters." Looking at the earl, feeling helpless, Violet exclaimed, "Do you see what I mean? I'm not really countess material, my lord."

"You'll be fine, Violet, I'm sure of it. You managed wonderfully before your husband passed. I witnessed it with my own eyes when I visited. You just need to get back in the habit."

"I suppose. If you'll excuse me."

The earl bowed to her as she left. His attention was gratifying. Violet only wished she wasn't too concerned about her niece to enjoy it.

Chapter Fifteen

L illian stood on the front step of the small house shifting from one foot to the other. There was no response to her multiple, loud knocks. She had even done the unthinkable and looked through the window. There was no sign of life within the dwelling. And all was quiet out of doors as well. She would have to go knock on her old home to ask about the residents.

After suiting her thoughts to actions, Lillian was no further ahead. No one there had any knowledge of the whereabouts of her old friend.

"I think she said something about going to visit her sister," was the vague response from the ragged woman who had opened the door. Lillian had been obliged to stifle her dismay over the disarray she could see had been made of her old home.

Checking with others in the small hamlet hadn't helped her much either. Many of her family's old friends were ill or away. Lillian was disappointed in herself for not having kept in better touch with their former neighbours. But they had really been friends of her parents. She had been a child; she shouldn't blame herself. But it now left her in a predicament.

She could, of course, make her way back to Ashburn Place. The grooms' apparent search for her let her know that she was welcome there, at least by the viscountess. But then what would she do? Shepley still wouldn't want her there. And even if Violet had been able to convince him to sponsor their Season, Lillian wasn't sure if she wanted one. An aristocratic marriage wasn't the ultimate solution her aunt seemed to think, in Lillian's opinion.

Lillian gazed down the road once more, indecision warring in her thoughts. She needed a position. Her eyes alighted on the sign of an inn just visible at the bend in the road. She was relieved there was more than one in the village. There was no way she could have returned to the first one where she had spoken of Ashburn Place and borrowed the innkeeper's stationery. She only hoped the other one needed help and would be willing to hire her without references. It wasn't the kind of position she had been hoping for, but she didn't have much choice.

Thirty minutes later, Lillian was once again standing on the street. The innkeeper wouldn't hire her. She couldn't say part of her wasn't relieved. It was a low place, and she would have been terrified. But a roof over her head would have been better than the barn she would have to make use of if she couldn't figure something out soon. The day was fast approaching its end.

Resolutely she turned her feet toward the big house of Sherton. Lillian had been hoping to approach the countess for her patronage for her bakery, not solicit a position as maid or kitchen help. With relief, Lillian remembered that she wouldn't actually have to speak with the countess about a position; she could approach the cook if she wanted a place in the kitchen, or the housekeeper if she was going to try her hand as maid. As she walked toward the House, she debated which position would be less onerous.

By the time she had arrived, she realized that the kitchens were the place for her. It would give her all the more experience for when she would gain her dowry and open her bakery. If she could practice baking, and if the countess enjoyed her work, she might be all the more willing to support her venture. And the kitchens would keep her away from any of the wellborn members of the household and provide fewer opportunities for awkwardness for anyone, herself included. The last thing she wanted was to run into someone she knew from her days at Ashburn Place.

Thus decided, her steps were not hesitant as she walked up the long driveway and went around back to the servants' entrance.

It was with much relief that Lillian was quickly welcomed into the household. She didn't want to rejoice over someone's misfortune, but it just so happened that several people had recently had to leave the earl's employ due to various familial tragedies, and the staff was relieved to add her to their number. They didn't ask too many questions, accepting at face value that she had been working at Ashburn Place and had wanted to return closer to home, not asking too much about where home was. Since Ashburn wasn't too very far away it was an acceptable story and she was hired on the spot and shown to her room. She would start first thing in the morning.

Lillian hadn't quite expected the day to end up like this. She had been hoping for a higher paid position, but at least she was to be the cook's assistant rather than a scullery maid. It paid slightly more, and from what she knew, the work was a little lighter. Lighter in weight only, but would also provide her much more training. All in all, she was reasonably happy with the outcome.

She was a little less happy about it when she was shaken awake a few hours later. It was still dark, and Lillian was momentarily confused.

"You'd best get a move on girl. Cook will turn you off if you're late."

"What?" Lillian asked groggily before it all rushed back to her. She quickly swung her feet over the side of the small bed she had slept in. Her sleep had been deep, even if it wasn't as long as she might have liked. The long walk and lack of sleep the night before meant she could have used a few more hours today, but that was a luxury she could not afford. She reminded herself to be grateful that she had been indoors and in a reasonably comfortable bed for the night. And she would be paid for whatever labours she did that day, she also reminded herself with a grin. It might not be much, but it would be all hers.

She had been provided a uniform of sorts the night before. After quickly donning it, she splashed water on her face from the cold water sitting on a table in the hallway and ran a comb through her hair before hurrying down to the kitchens just as the cook entered the room.

Lillian was relieved not to be yelled at first thing and whispered a prayer of thanks for the girl who had thought to wake her. She hadn't even given her name. Lillian would have to seek her out later.

The day flew by as she chopped, sliced, stirred, and tasted each dish as she followed the cook's bellowed directions. He might be a drill sergeant, but he was an excellent cook. Lillian was satisfied that the experience would be of benefit to her. Even though the pay would be lower, she would be better off here than following the whims of some crotchety old woman as her aunt had said.

The kitchen staff was allowed to end their day earlier than some of the other servants, much to Lillian's relief. As the cook's assistant, she could quit when he did, since they per force had to start early, as well. She climbed the many floors up to the servants' quarters feeling every muscle in her body protesting the experiences of the day. But there was a smile on her face despite her many aches. It had been a good day.

Lillian reminded herself that she ought to write to let her aunt know she had found a position, but she wasn't sure how she would be able to accomplish that. She would have a day off at the end of the week. Perhaps she could return to the inn where she had written her first letter. But there was no groom waiting to take her note. She would have to pay for postage.

But it could not be helped. She couldn't leave her aunt to fret. It was also not something she had to worry about at this moment. Lillian made quick work of wiping away the sweat from the day and climbing into bed. She didn't have the energy for anything else. It would be morning before she knew it.

The days soon melded into a routine and passed quickly. Before she knew it, her half-day off had arrived. She only had to help with the breakfast preparations and then had the rest of the day to herself. Of course, since she had to rise so early, Lillian knew she couldn't spend too much time dithering, but she was delighted to be out of doors and in the sunshine. That was the worst drawback of her position. She almost never saw the sun. She arose before the sun did and spent the entire day in the kitchen, rarely setting foot out of doors before returning to her bed in the attics just as the sun was setting.

Chapter Sixteen

"Still nothing?" Violet couldn't believe her niece had just disappeared off the face of the earth. "She must have been abducted. There is no other possibility."

"Now, my lady, you must calm yourself. It will do nothing good to find yourself in a taking."

"Do not tell me to calm myself." Even as she said it, Violet could hear how shrill her tone was. She tried to soften it by smiling at the housekeeper. "I know you are only trying to help, Mrs. Parker, but I cannot find it in me to be calm. My only living relative is missing, and it's all my fault."

"Now, my lady, you certainly must know that isn't entirely true. Yes, perhaps you could have helped the girl find a position, but she's the one who took it into her mind to walk through the night in an attempt to look after herself. You never asked the girl to be so ridiculously independent."

"But I let her become that way."

"Were her parents nothing like that, my lady?"

Violet hesitated. The housekeeper wasn't wrong. Violet's darling brother, Lillian's father, had been independent to a fault, as well. He had insisted, as soon as he was able, to get a position as the blacksmith's apprentice. It had not been what was expected of a gently born young man, but as he had said, "Being gently born will not put food on the family's table, as far as I can see." Lillian had the very same attitude. She couldn't bear to wait around hoping someone else would provide for her. She was determined to provide for herself. Violet supposed it was an admirable quality. But right at this moment she wanted to wring that quality right out of her dear niece.

"Why hasn't she sent word?"

"Perhaps she is too busy?"

"It isn't like her to leave me to worry," Violet insisted. "Something dreadful has surely befallen the girl."

"Perhaps she considers that she did send word, my lady. With the groom. She told you she was going to find a position and for you not to fret."

"But she also said she would let me know where she ended up."

"If she found a position, she might not have the time or circumstances to write to you. I can't even imagine where I'd look if one of the maids asked me to frank a letter for them in their first week of employment."

Violet looked at the housekeeper with dismay. "But surely, if she is the companion to some gentlewoman, she could just tell the butler to add it to the household post."

"How was the girl to find a gentlewoman to be companion to, my lady?" It was apparent to Violet that the housekeeper had tried to be gentle as she said it, but Violet felt as though she had been slapped nonetheless.

"So, what kind of a position do you think my niece has found?" Violet could hear the horror in her voice and hoped the housekeeper didn't take offence, but with her head filling with images of her niece working herself to flinders, she couldn't find it in herself to think of other's feelings.

"Miss Lillian is the most capable young woman I have ever had the pleasure to meet. She will be successful in whatever position she could possibly land. And she has the sense to find one that won't be too far outside of her realm."

"So, you don't think she's cleaning out someone's latrine as we speak?"

The housekeeper chuckled. "I do not, and you shouldn't either, my lady. You will hear from her in good time. I am certain of it."

Violet wasn't so certain, but she couldn't stand around wringing her hands much longer. The skin was already going to be raw from her lamenting thus far. The earl was awaiting her upon his estate after having stayed the extra day with her, as he had offered. She knew he had wanted to relieve her mind and stay even longer, but he hadn't wanted to remain there with his impressionable, young daughter. Violet couldn't blame him. She hadn't been in any frame of mind to entertain anyway, certainly not the sweet, young girl that could potentially be a stepdaughter.

With her heart twisting as she thought of that sweet, young woman, Violet couldn't help comparing her with her niece and wasn't sure which was better. While she was currently nearly out of her mind with worry over her niece because of her stubborn independence, she wouldn't trade her in for anything. And the earl's daughter's sweet passivity made it a little challenging to keep a conversation going. But the young woman was no trouble at all.

Violet immediately felt disloyal for the thought. Her niece had been nothing but supportive toward her since the viscount died. She was only causing her trouble because Violet loved her so much and was worried. It wasn't Lillian's fault she had been banished. Well, perhaps it was a little bit. Violet had never gotten a firm explanation as to why the girl was in the steward's office in the first place. Lester hadn't known, nor cared, why she was there, merely seeing it as the excuse he had been looking for to get rid of the girl. It was the first thing she would ask her niece as soon as she was located.

Pacing was doing her no good. Violet was just thinking of ringing for a carriage to be prepared for her so she could go to Sherton herself and look around for the girl. She used to live there herself; surely she could find some old friends who might know something. Suddenly, her attention was drawn to the sounds of a bit of commotion at the front of the house.

"My lord, I would ask that you wait here while I see if her ladyship is receiving."

At the sound of the butler addressing someone as 'my lord,' Violet's heartbeat sped up, thinking it might be her Leopold, but the next words made her frown. It was clearly not Lord Avery.

"Be quick about it, man."

How rude, Violet thought as she waited for a servant to appear.

"My lady, I'm sorry to disturb you, but the Earl of Sedgwick is here to see you."

"The Earl of Sedgwick?" she repeated, as though to ascertain if she had heard correctly. "How very strange. Very well, you may show him in."

The butler must not have been able to return all the way to the front of the house because it was only seconds later that the earl burst into the room.

"My lady, a pleasure to see you."

Violet felt her eyes widen. The somewhat distracted young man she remembered from the house party was gone. In his place, he was just as handsome, perhaps even more so, as he watched her with an alert, intelligent gaze. If Lillian had ever seen him like this, Violet was no longer surprised that she had been distracted by the man. She felt her lips tip up into a wide smile.

"The pleasure is mine, my lord. To what do I owe the pleasure of a visit from you? I don't think we're so very near Sedgwick, here at Ashburn, are we, my lord?"

"No, my lady, I came specifically to see you. Or rather, your niece."

Violet felt equal portions of dismay and delight well up in her chest. She could not produce her niece, but she was thrilled that an eligible young man was asking for her.

"I'm sorry to say that my niece is unavailable to visit today."

"So, Shepley followed through on his threat to evict her, did he? I knew it. I should never have left here without making sure she was going to be all right."

Violet stiffened. "I don't know what you're talking about, my lord."

His eyes narrowed on her. "Then I will wait until Miss Shaw is available."

"You cannot wait here. That would be highly irregular."

"Why not? I was Shepley's guest just last week."

Violet blinked at the earl. While what he was doing was, as she had said, irregular, he wasn't wrong about the fact that Lester probably wouldn't mind him being there. But her stepson would be sure to tell him that he had, in fact, banished the girl. Lillian was going to be ruined. Her doting aunt didn't know what to do. Helpless tears threatened, and she blinked to hold them back.

She must not have hidden them well, though, as the earl's gaze sharpened noticeably. But his face also softened.

"I apologize, my lady, I have no wish to make you uncomfortable. I just need to be reassured that Lillian has not fared badly from her association with me."

"With you? What do you have to do with anything?"

She was fascinated by the colour that splashed along his cheeks. "I would rather not say, my lady, but I need to know that she is all right."

Now it was Violet's turn to sharpen her gaze on her guest. "What have you done to my niece, my lord?"

"I haven't done anything to her, I promise you. Could you not, please, tell me where she is so that I might speak with her, even briefly?"

"It is not possible at the moment, my lord."

"What is not possible? I cannot speak with her or you cannot tell me where she is?"

Violet bit her lip, indecision warring within her. "What are your intentions toward my niece, my lord? It is most unusual for a nobleman to be quite so insistent upon seeing a young woman."

The colour returned to the earl's cheeks, but he didn't back down. "I promise you, my intentions are acceptable. Well, I would hope they are acceptable to her. I would like to pay her my addresses."

Violet wanted to do a little dance to express her delight but restrained herself to clapping her hands. She quickly sobered though. Eyeing him with as serious an expression as she could muster upon her face, Violet asked, "Can I trust you, my lord?"

"Of course," he sounded offended.

"Do not take offence. I barely know you. And my niece's future hangs in the balance."

The earl took a deep breath before offering her a sweet smile. "I can assure you, my lady, that I would like nothing better than to ensure a beautiful future for your niece."

Violet blinked at him. "Is this not a very sudden change, my lord? I know nothing of you developing feelings for my niece while you were here. And she is not someone who would typically be pursued by an earl, since she is neither a noble, nor a great heiress."

"I don't need either. And yes, I can see that it may appear sudden, but I can assure you it is not." He paused for a moment. "Well, perhaps it is when you consider that we actually met less than a month ago. If not for the fact that I am aware of the threats Shepley made a week ago, I would probably not be here making a declaration at this time, but I could not rest easy worrying about her."

"I still wonder how you know about those threats, but I will tell you that she considered them more than threats. She left here that night, and I haven't seen her since. She left me a letter before she walked away and sent another letter through the groom I sent to fetch her, but I haven't seen her since the last evening of the house party."

The earl nodded. "I was afraid of that. She is far too stubborn for her own good." He looked at Violet, and she saw what appeared to be desperation in his gaze. "Do you know where she went?"

"She was last seen in Sherton, but I haven't heard from her since. And I have been hesitating about launching an actual search for fear of damaging her reputation. You see, I have procured the offer of a Season for the two of us. I don't want her chances marred by any knowledge of this mix up."

"It seems like more than a mix up, my lady. And if I have my way, she won't need a Season."

"She might not need it, but every young lady deserves to know a Season."

The earl laughed. "This is not a subject I wish to debate with you at the moment. Shall we agree that Miss Shaw can decide whether or not she wants a Season once we have ensured her safety?"

Violet beamed at him, delighted with his obvious concern for her niece. "Very well, my lord. What do you intend to do?"

"I shall start in Sherton and not stop until I've found the girl."

"And will you bring her to me?"

"Not necessarily. I have no desire to subject her to Lester's presence ever again. Could you perhaps have a bag packed and be prepared to remove from here? If she will agree to take me, there is nothing questionable about the two of you visiting my estate."

Violet's eyes widened. "We have also been invited for an extended visit to Lord Avery's estate. I will pack for both of us. Do you think you will have her today?"

"I will do my very best, my lady, but for that, I shall have to bid you farewell for the moment."

"Yes, of course, please, think nothing of me. Can I send some servants with you? They could help. And they could bring me information."

The earl grinned. "You must have been beside yourself to be here without knowing anything for the past week."

"You have no idea."

"Very well, one servant. I don't want to draw undue attention, as you say, to Miss Shaw's circumstances. But it might be useful to be able to contact you if needed."

"Thank you, my lord. I promise, the servants are well trained and shan't interfere with whatever you need to do."

Chapter Seventeen

A s he rode away, the earl thought about what had brought him to this time and place.

Brock had ridden out of London early the morning after he had seen his overseer at the theater. The morning was glorious, and he had been thrilled to leave the stench of the city behind.

As he rode, his mind wandered over all the events of the past weeks. At times he found himself grinning like a simpleton over certain things Miss Shaw had said. She was such an interesting mix. At times sweet and funny, always working hard. He had never met a young woman like her. She didn't have the subservience of a servant nor the haughtiness of a debutante. He rather liked her and was hard pressed to get her out of his mind.

He tried to distract himself with thoughts of all that he wanted to accomplish at Sedgwick, but even there, the girl was intruding into his thoughts as he remembered the scene when he had tried to convince her he was examining the woodwork and not searching Lester's study. Brock laughed out loud over the memory. Any other well-bred woman would have accepted his words. A servant wouldn't have believed him but would have been too nervous to contradict him. Not his Lillian. She had strode right in and called him on his lies.

Not that it did her any good. Her intelligence had gotten her caught up in his investigation, which had led to her banishment from the only home she had. Foolish girl. Brock hoped she had learned from the experience and managed to keep a firmer hold on her curiosity in the future and remained in the role she was supposed to be filling. No one would keep a companion around who couldn't remain in her place, he was certain.

The earl tried once more to think of other things and finally was able to do so when his estate came into view. He had never expected to inherit and would never have wished his brother ill, but he had always loved the old pile of bricks and was proud beyond measure to be able to call it his.

A couple days passed while he saw to estate business. He had been gone nearly a month, and there were still things to see to from before he inherited. His father and brother had allowed the estate to get run down, and he would have plenty of work in the coming months and years to get it back to the top shape it ought to be. Brock thought of Lillian once more and what she would be able to accomplish if she were steward or housekeeper at Sedgwick as she had asked him. Of course, he could never bring her here in such a role, but he knew she would thrive if he could.

Once he thought of her in his home, he couldn't push the idea away. And his concern over what had become of her started to hang heavy over him. It was his fault she had been in that study. Brock wasn't certain what had made the steward suspicious. He wasn't sure the man ever set foot in his office in the evening. Or any time, if he could avoid it, the cur was a lazy bag of bones that was exploiting the viscount. But Brock wasn't wasting any concern for Lester. The wastrel had banished a young woman who, by rights, should have been under his care.

She really wasn't Brock's responsibility, but he couldn't quite convince himself of that. The more he thought of her, the more he wanted to think about her. He couldn't dismiss from his mind images of her, dressed properly as befit a young woman of her station, gracing his breakfast room with her presence, or bustling about the house getting it into order. When he was also picturing her in his bedroom, he knew he was done for and the only thing left for him to do was go and find her. He was hoping beyond hope that her aunt had stepped in and prevented her from actually leaving Ashburn Place, so he would start there in his search for his future countess.

This was how he found himself standing outside Ashburn Place with a clammy hand raised toward the knocker. He wondered if his handlers *had brought their investigation yet. Brock wasn't sure what sort of reception he would receive. Since he had been adamant that he was retiring from the Home Office, they might not be too concerned about protecting his identity. Of course, they would prefer to prevent scandal, even if they didn't care about looking out for him, so he should be safe as far as that goes. And it had always been Lillian who had caught him out. Neither Shepley nor the steward had any knowledge of his searches. His heart swelled in pride as he remembered how Lillian had accepted Lester's decree without plea or any mention of Brock and his search. She would be a remarkable partner for his future endeavours, whatever they might be.*

Finally, with resolution, he brought the knocker down firmly. The door was quickly wrenched open by the butler he remembered from his visit.

"My lord," the usually contained older servant gazed at him as though uncertain of his role.

"Good afternoon, I would like to speak with Lady Shepley."

Brock was making quick work of riding to Sherton after his interview with the viscountess. He tried to quell his concern for Lillian, but the fact that she hadn't sent word to her aunt filled him with dismay. He knew she would never want to cause concern for her only relative. He agreed with Violet that the only reason the girl had left was to spare the viscountess' feelings when faced with a houseful of noble guests. It was foolish on the girl's part, of course, and he would tell her so as soon as he found her safe.

If he found her safe. Brock felt more fear than on any previous occasion as he rode into the small hamlet a little more than ten miles from Ashburn. It was ridiculous, really. He had faced blades, fists, and crowds, all without batting an eye. Now, as he worried about the girl, he felt as though his heart were going to pound out of his chest. What if he couldn't find her? What if, while he was dithering, something dreadful had befallen her? Would she ever forgive him? Would he ever forgive himself?

He made his first stop at the inn where the Ashburn groom had said she had written the letter to her aunt.

"My lord, it is an honour to have you stop by our humble establishment."

The innkeeper's enthusiasm made Brock smile, at least slightly. He wondered if Lillian received the same welcome. That sobered him.

"I am looking for a young woman who came through here about a week ago. She was from Ashburn Place and needed to write a letter to her aunt. Do you recall?"

The innkeeper eyed him with speculation gleaming in his eyes. "We value our patrons' privacy here, my lord. I am not certain I should tell you anything about a previous visitor."

Brock gritted his teeth. "How about you bring me a tankard and one for yourself, and we'll see if we can remember between us when last you might have seen the girl."

The innkeeper, as Brock knew he would, grinned with delight over the promise of coins. After he poured them each a drink, the man leaned in closer.

"I shouldn't normally speak of my patrons, but if you're looking for her, I should tell you, since she might be in some sort of danger, a young girl on her own."

"Was she on her own?"

"Well, no, she had her groom with her, of course. But she told me some Banbury story about her aunt, but no one has come by from Ashburn Place in weeks."

"And you haven't seen the girl since?"

"No, my lord, I haven't. Although I thought I saw her earlier today, but it was just a resemblance."

Brock forced a grin. "Blonde young women are thick on the ground, aren't they?"

The innkeeper wasn't wrong. From a distance, many of the young women looked similar. But not his Lillian. How anyone could mistake her for someone else would be a mystery to Brock.

Brock tossed back the rest of his drink and flicked the innkeeper his coin before striding out of the room. Lillian wasn't here, that was certain. Perhaps he would have more luck at the other inn he could just see before the road bent.

A matronly woman answered his summons, but she didn't appear willing to share any information about any young women.

"Can't be divulging anything I might know about any young women, my lord. And don't bother shaking your purse at me. I've got me some standards. And protecting girls is one of 'em. I'll thank you to get yourself off my front porch unless you're needing a room."

Brock couldn't prevent a kernel of respect that germinated in his chest. He appreciated the woman's fortitude in refusing to be bought off.

"I might need a room for the night. I won't be sure until I've asked around a little bit more. Thank you for your time."

The buxom older woman just sniffed at him, and Brock laughed as he walked back to his horse. Lady Violet had given him the direction of Lillian's former residence. He would start by asking the neighbours if they had seen her. Violet was certain she hadn't had success with any of them, or she would have sent word, but by now she may have been able to make contact.

Frustration was growing within him as one by one he was met with silence. Either there was no one home or they didn't know what he was talking about. He was gratified by the reactions of the few people he had found who remembered her. Every last one of them had nothing but good things to say about Lillian and her family.

"You be sure to give my love when you find her," the last woman had said. "I only wish I had been here to receive her myself."

Brock hadn't wanted to tell the full story and had kept most of the details to himself, but he had been forced to divulge some information to the people he was questioning, as they had become defensive and protective when he had been asking around about Lillian Shaw.

"What's it to you, my lord? Miss Shaw is a special young woman and not to be trifled with," had been the reaction at one door.

"Of course, of course, my good woman. I mean her no ill, I promise you. But she found herself in a bit of a needful situation and was looking for somewhere to stay. I have news from her aunt and am trying to find her so she can come home."

"Oh, the poor dear. I'm right sorry that I can't say I was able to help the poor dear in her moment of need."

When the older woman began to weep Brock became truly uncomfortable. He awkwardly patted her on the shoulder. "I am certain she is fine. If you remember her well, you know how resourceful the girl is."

This seemed to be the right thing to say. The older woman's tears slowed, and she was able to smile. "That she certainly is, the sweet, dear girl."

"I'll be sure to give her your greetings when I find her."

"Thank you, my lord. Perhaps you could tell her to write a letter to me?"

"I will mention it," he promised as he silently reprimanded himself for wondering if the woman knew how to read. He couldn't imagine his Lillian living in surroundings like these. Of course, the house next door, the one that had belonged to her family was slightly better. It was showing signs of wear now, but it appeared to have been well cared for up until recently. If he recalled correctly, Lillian's parents had been ill before their deaths, so they probably hadn't been able to keep it perfectly even while they lived there. Knowing his Lillian, though, she would have done her best to keep it all together.

He was able to excuse himself from the neighbour and continue on his search. He was just about to knock on another door when he heard a voice from behind him.

"I hear you're looking for me."

Brock whirled around, almost losing his balance. He felt heat spread across his face as she laughed at him.

"Where have you been?" he almost bellowed.

"It's nice to see you, too," Lillian replied back to him with a smirk. "Could we perhaps not have this conversation on the street? I only have a couple hours free, and I have much I need to accomplish."

Brock's eyebrows rose to his hairline. The girl had most definitely not been cowed by her recent experiences.

"You look well."

"Thank you, did you think I had been ill?"

"Your aunt has been looking for you. She was worried. I've been worried."

He felt her eyes searching his face but wasn't over his anger enough to reassure her.

"My aunt had no reason to be worried. I informed her of my intentions, not only once, but twice."

"But apparently you said in your second message that you would let her know your direction."

"Did she expect it immediately? I haven't been free to do so. In fact, I had just gone to the inn to write to her when I was told a fancy lord was searching for me. I will have you know, I don't appreciate you wandering around town speaking about me. It will do nothing good for my reputation."

Brock blinked at her, surprised by her reaction.

"As I said, we were worried."

"What did you think had happened to me?"

"All sorts of bad things could have befallen you, Lillian. I don't want to sully your innocent ears with details, but there are bad men who would like nothing better than to get their hands on a beautiful young woman like you."

The earl was relieved to see she responded to his words, but then she quickly reacted in a way he would not have expected, although on second thought, he should have.

Lillian burst into laughter. "Thank you for that, my lord. I have been far too serious for the past week. I needed a good laugh. Yes, I am well aware that bad things happen. Especially to good people, it would seem from what I've seen of life. But I was taught from a very young age how to protect myself." She held up a hand to stem whatever he was about to say. "I know, I know, I'm small and female and thus unable to truly look after myself, or at least in the opinion of most men. But I'm not stupid. Yes, it might have been foolish to walk away from Ashburn in the middle of the night, I realized that in hindsight, but by the time I did, I was halfway to Sherton. My options were to continue on, or to return. They were fairly equal in their risk, so I carried on. And sent word to my aunt when the groom found me. Written word, in fact, to make sure the poor groom didn't get into any trouble. So I was not negligent, nor foolhardy. I have been safe and sound at Sherton House almost from the moment I walked into the village."

"But as a servant? Really, Lillian? That is what you have aspired to accomplish with your life?"

"There is nothing wrong with good, honest labour, my lord. I would far prefer working hard for my living than searching through a fellow nobleman's private papers, I can assure you."

Brock felt the heat climb in his cheeks once more. He was momentarily at a loss for words. Lillian filled the silence.

"Now that you've seen for yourself that I am fine, although, now that I'm saying that, I am left to wonder how you even came to the conclusion that you needed to be concerned about me. It has been more than a week since you overheard Lester evict me from my home and did nothing to help me. Did it take that long for your conscience to prod you?"

When Brock opened his mouth and nothing came out, Lillian plowed on.

"Never mind, allow your conscience to absolve you, my lord. I am actually perfectly happy in my position here at Sherton. The cook is brilliant, and I am more than capable of keeping up with his demands. I will be in an excellent position to start my bakery when I inherit. And I will be an unmitigated success."

Brock had to smile over her words. "I'm absolutely certain you will be, too, but I *was* worried about you."

Her expression was quizzical. "That's nice, of you, I suppose. I never meant to worry anyone, much less you. I didn't think you had even given me a moment's thought, to be perfectly honest. So, thank you for acting on your concern. I suppose if something truly had befallen me, I would appreciate your pursuit of me. But you can see that I'm perfectly fine. And actually, since you're here, and you have clearly spoken to my aunt, you could take the message to her that I am fine and am well ensconced here at Sherton House. This way she needn't worry anymore, and I don't have to go to the expense of posting a letter to her."

He felt like a simpleton, but Brock could only blink at her. "You intend to remain here?"

"Well, of course, where else am I to go? You, yourself, heard Shepley say how very unwelcome I am at Ashburn."

"Yes, of course, I forgot, in all the excitement of finding you, to tell you that your aunt has made arrangements. You are to have your Season. I think the earl, Lord Avery, is pursuing a courtship with her. You are to accompany her to visit his estate."

He grew uncomfortable under her steady stare when she didn't say anything. He could almost see the workings of her brain as she pondered his words. He hurried into more speech.

"I apologize, Lillian, you asked that we not stand here on the road talking, and yet that is what I have allowed to happen. Could I escort you back to the inn and we could have a small repast?"

She still didn't say anything but nodded and fell into step beside him as they walked back toward the inn. Brock wasn't sure which of the inns he should go to. The first one, whose owner already knew her as being from Ashburn, or the other one where the innkeeper knew her as a servant. Neither would be good for her reputation if she insisted upon remaining in Sherton.

"I didn't realize my aunt would still expect me to remain with her." She finally spoke. Her quiet tone caused him concern. She sounded deeply disappointed.

"Why does this make you sad? Aren't you glad she still wants your company?"

"Lord Sedgwick, don't you realize that I am solely responsible for myself? My parents were unable to leave me much in a material way. To be blunt, I am impoverished. Yes, my aunt is a viscountess, but her husband didn't leave her truly well provided for. He had no intention of dying, of course, so I cannot be angry with him, but he must have known what a lout Lester is, so he shouldn't have left his wife in a position of being dependent on that wastrel's good will. She has a small stipend, of course, but it isn't enough to set her up independently of Ashburn. And it certainly isn't enough to provide for the two of us."

"But there are other options for you now."

151

"Like what? I don't want her to remarry just to provide for me. I am perfectly capable of providing for myself. I have a position now. Yes, the pay is low, but I actually enjoy the work. I will be well placed and trained to run my bakery when I receive the bequest. I shall be just fine on my own. But if Violet needs me, then I will go to her. If she truly wants to go stay with Lord Avery. Not if she's doing it in a misguided sense of providing for me."

"I see," Brock said, although he truly didn't. He had never met a woman so determined to be independent. "Perhaps she just misses you."

He regretted his words as soon as she turned tear-filled eyes toward him. "Well, I miss her, too, but being here pays me. Being with her, I work almost as hard but don't get paid." She held up her hand quickly. "Please don't misunderstand, I love being with my aunt and truly loved running Ashburn Place. If I could be hired as a steward somewhere, I would leave here in a heartbeat. I would even give up my idea of a bakery, as running an estate is more fulfilling, I think, and more to my temperament." She paused again, replacing her tear-filled eyes with a grin. "To be honest with you, I'm not completely certain how I'm going to handle customers."

Brock returned her grin, but before he could respond she carried on. "But the fact remains that no one is going to hire a woman as their steward. And my background makes it so that it's probably just as impossible to be hired as a housekeeper. The only reason I was hired at Sherton is because it was the cook doing the hiring, and he didn't ask too many questions. At least not about my family. He just wanted to know if I knew my way around the kitchen."

Finally, Brock was able to stem the flow of her words. "But there are other options. What about a Season? If you find a husband, you'll have an estate to run, just as you'd like."

"But what if I don't? I'm unconventional, to say the least, my lord. There's no guarantee I'll find a husband willing to take me on. And I don't want to be tied for life to someone who will merely tolerate me, or worse, expect me to be different than I am. No, I think it is far better to stay where I am. If it doesn't work out, I can find something else. Once you're married, it's for life. And I would hate to have to be waiting for a husband to conveniently pass on so that I can benefit from his demise."

"What if you could be guaranteed that your husband would think you're the best thing that ever happened to him?"

Lillian snorted. By then, they had reached the inn yard. Brock pulled her behind the hedge that was lining the property, affording them a degree of privacy.

"I'm serious, Lillian."

"No one but my parents has ever thought I was the best thing that ever happened to them, my lord."

"Why will you never call me by name?"

"I'm in service now, my lord, it's not seemly."

Brock grinned at her prim tone before returning to the subject at hand. "But what if? Would you consider it? Or are you so determined to remain independent that you have no wish to wed, no matter who the groom might be?"

Now she was searching his face as he invaded her space, far too close for what she would, of course, consider seemly, but she didn't push him away, much to the earl's relief.

"What are you trying to say, my lord? It isn't kind to dangle fairy tales before me. I have chosen my path, and I believe it is the best one for me."

"I think that meeting you was the best thing that has ever happened to me, and I would be eternally grateful if you would consent to be my wife."

Chapter Eighteen

Lillian stared up into the handsome face before her. Her heart galloped. There was no other word for it. It actually made her feel faint for the briefest moment. She frowned. And then quickly burst into laughter at the disappointment that flooded the earl's face. Before she could speak, he stepped away from her.

"Of course, you cannot imagine the drudgery of marrying me. You would far rather bake crumpets for the Earl of Sherton. The very married Earl of Sherton, I might add."

"Are you finished, my lord?"

Her tart tone brought his gaze back to her face, and she was gratified by the eager expression she saw there.

"I have no particular desire to remain in the Earl of Sherton's household, I can assure you. It was the first paid position that presented itself. Well, rather, there were two options. I decided that working in the kitchens was preferable to being a chambermaid."

"Wise choice, I should say. Very few chamber pots in the kitchens."

"That was exactly my thoughts, my lord. Besides the fact that it is extremely rare that the gently born enter the kitchens, so there is far less opportunity for awkward encounters with people I might have met previously."

"That is also a consideration I would not have thought of, but sensible of you to analyse."

Lillian couldn't contain her grin. She had missed these bantering conversations. But she quickly sobered. She had some contentions to raise with the earl.

"You left me to fend for myself, my lord."

"A fact for which I will be eternally ashamed." The expression on his face was entirely sincere. Lillian couldn't detect even a hint of amusement. She believed him.

"You stood behind the curtains and allowed Lester to banish me."

"I did. I regretted it from the instant it was happening. But you do realize I had a mission to accomplish."

"What would you have done if you didn't?"

"Well, I wouldn't have even met you, if not for the mission. There are no circumstances in this lifetime that would have prevailed upon me to spend any time in Shepley's company, let alone attend a house party at Ashburn."

"Now you're just being logical, my lord. Suppose for a moment. If not for the mission, what would you have done?"

"I would have faced the scandal and stood by your side."

"What scandal?"

"The one that would have ensued from the two of us being discovered in the steward's office alone."

"Oh, well, yes, of course."

"And then I would have declared that you had made me the happiest man in the realm by agreeing to be my wife."

"But you hadn't asked."

"Being in the steward's office alone with me was my way of asking."

"In our pretend scenario, you mean?"

"Yes, in all reality, I'm standing behind the hedge of a common inn to ask."

Lillian's grin returned. So did the butterflies in her stomach. And her heartbeat quickened, but she was able to keep her head.

"I'm not a lady, you know."

"You will be."

"I haven't much of a dowry."

"I don't need one. I'm quite wealthy on my own, I can assure you. You can keep your ten pounds. I'll teach you how to invest."

"Truly?"

"Really and truly. I think you'll be quite good at it."

Lillian grinned but then eyed him carefully. "If I agree, you will have to provide for me properly in your Will. I don't think anyone will hire a former countess to work in their kitchens."

"I vow to you, Lillian Shaw, that if you will marry me, you will never lack for anything for the rest of your days, whether I am alive or not."

Lillian bit on her lip, trying to decide.

"Your offer is a good one, my lord, and I recognize the honour you are bestowing upon me by making it, but I'm not sure if I ought to accept."

The incredulous expression on his face would have been amusing if not for the serious nature of their conversation. Lillian couldn't even smile at him. She felt tears threaten.

"Don't cry, my dear. I have no desire to make you uncomfortable, I swear it. Please, tell me why you're hesitating. It's almost certain I haven't expressed myself properly, despite my supposed abilities."

This finally made her laugh, even if it was a little watery.

"You haven't said anything about your feelings, Brock. Do you even WANT me to be your wife? Is it just because you feel badly that I got banished for helping you?"

"Good heavens, no. I'd be married ten times over if I had wed with any person I felt badly about in my investigations. Did I fail to mention that I've fallen desperately in love with you?"

"Yes, you arrogant buffoon. Did you think I would read your mind?"

"Forgive me, please, my darling," he said as he laughed and pulled her into his arms. "I desperately want you as my wife. I fought the feelings for a week but couldn't get you out of my mind. I want you in my house, in my life, in my study, in my bed. To be honest with you, I would like it if you could just glue yourself to my side, but I know that isn't a practical suggestion. Just marry me. I will be miserable without you. Please, I'll beg if I must."

Lillian gazed up at him, a difficult task considering he was trying to tuck her under his chin. She was trying to gauge his sincerity.

"Do you truly mean it?"

"It is the most sincere declaration I have made in my entire life."

"Very well then. Just to ensure you aren't miserable for all eternity, I will accept, thank you, my lord."

He threw back his head and laughed until tears started to form in his eyes. "Life with you will never be dull, will it?"

She grinned in return until his face turned serious.

"Are you just accepting so you needn't be a cook's assistant?"

"Are you jesting with me? I quite like being the cook's assistant. The fact that a countess is most likely not allowed in the kitchen is one of the things which make me hesitate to accept, if you must know."

"Then what made you accept?"

"Well, for one thing, I don't really want my aunt to marry Lord Avery just to provide for me."

"You probably could have talked her out of that."

Lillian nodded. "That's true. But you have promised me an entire estate to manage, that sounds deliciously entertaining."

"If that's all you wanted, perhaps your aunt could have found someone who needed a companion to run their lives."

"That's quite true, except that Lady Violet has assured me that such ladies must be frightfully dreadful company."

"There is that, of course." The earl finally seemed to realize she was teasing him and relaxed back against the barn, holding her comfortably in his arms, a smile growing on his face. Lillian relaxed, too. She felt as though she could comfortably remain standing just like that for the rest of her life. But since he had been brave enough to tell her his feelings, she ought to do the same for him.

"But even more than your estate, I find that I, too, would like to be by your side for the rest of eternity, my lord. I do trust you have no intention of leaving me a widow any time soon. I swear, I'll never forgive you if you do."

"And why is that?"

"Because I am quite desperately in love with you and couldn't bear it if you were to abandon me to life without you."

The smile that spread across his face caused the breath to hitch in her throat. But then all her breath left her as his head descended and his lips settled over hers. She knew she had made the right decision. Despite all practicalities, they were to have a love match. Lillian congratulated herself on the accomplishment before all thought fled her mind and she threw herself enthusiastically into their first of many passionate kisses.

Epilogue

Lillian fought back tears as she watched her aunt's maid put the finishing touches on her hair. Lady Violet had never looked more beautiful. Lily was delighted that her aunt had found joy with a new partner, and she was certain Uncle Wilbur would have been happy for all of them. He was not the sort who would begrudge anyone happiness. If he could no longer be there to care for his beloved wife, Lillian was certain the viscount would be relieved that his old friend would do so. And Lillian was convinced that Lord Avery was going to do a very good job of it.

She hadn't yet gotten to the point of being comfortable enough to address him by anything other than Lord Avery or even just Avery, but the earl had made every effort to welcome her into his home. Lillian was surprised that the serious older man had actually been so generous and open to having her there after Sedgwick had found her at Sherton and returned her to Ashburn Place.

Of course, Brock hadn't wanted her to become ensconced with Avery, but it wasn't as if Lillian could go and stay at Sedgwick. Aunt Violet had been torn trying to please both noblemen. Lillian had been forced to put her foot down and insist that they stay with Avery until her aunt's marriage. Thankfully, the older earl had insisted he wanted as short a betrothal as possible without causing a scandal.

Choking back a watery chuckle, Lillian recalled how happy the earl was that it was a Friday when she and Violet had shown up on his doorstep in the company of Lord Sedgwick.

"Excellent. The banns can be read on Sunday," he had declared with a sense of satisfaction that first evening.

Now here they were, just a little over two weeks later, but the banns had been read the requisite three times. The third time being the day before in the small chapel in which Lillian would be pleased to watch her beloved aunt pledge herself to the handsome earl.

Then chaos would ensue. Sedgwick had been wishing to bring her back to his estate, but Aunt Violet had been surprisingly resistant. She had insisted that Lillian was owed at least a taste of a Season before she committed herself to life as a countess. Sedgwick had growled and grumbled but had finally agreed. Thankfully, the fall session wasn't too far off.

Kathryn, Violet's soon to be new stepdaughter, was reacting very well to the disruption of her quiet life. Lillian had enjoyed getting to know the young woman over the past two weeks and was relieved that the earl had stopped watching their interactions so suspiciously. Violet had whispered to Lillian that Avery had wished to send her to one of his married children to protect Kathryn's innocence from Lillian but that Violet had been able to prevail upon him to get to know her niece before casting judgment.

Despite his arranging for the banns to be read within days of her arrival, Violet had insisted that Avery collect the rest of his family to his estate to meet her before she would actually agree to the marriage. Lillian was impressed and delighted to see her aunt blossoming back into the strong woman she had been before she had lost her first husband.

Thankfully, Avery's older daughter and son both welcomed Violet and Lillian into their lives without many qualms. They were preoccupied with their own lives but gracious enough to be glad for their father's happiness. So finally, after the second reading of the banns, Violet had agreed to marry the earl, to his relief and everyone else's amusement. The last week had been a flurry of activity as the estate was scrubbed from top to bottom and everything prepared to celebrate.

Lillian had itched to take control of the preparations but forced herself to remain in the background. This would never be her home, and it was best that Violet feel her own way forward. Her aunt had consulted with her on numerous things, but it was obvious to Lillian that she wouldn't be needed in the future. Avery's staff was competent, and Aunt Violet was becoming accustomed to resuming control.

Brock had come and gone with alarming regularity. Alarming because Lillian struggled with the depths of her longing for his company whenever he was absent. But, as he pointed out, he needed to set a few things in motion upon his own estate before they settled there. And, as he further pointed out with a glower, if he was to dance attendance upon her during at least a part of the Season.

And they were all to adjourn to Sedgwick for two weeks during the middle of August so Lillian and Brock could spend time together on his home front. Lillian couldn't wait. While she was looking forward to a week of quiet after the wedding while Violet and Leopold went to his hunting lodge and she remained behind with Kathryn, Brock was to absent himself so she was sure to be lonely despite the younger woman's chattering company.

"How do I look?"

Violet's question pulled Lillian from her troubled thoughts, and she turned to her aunt with a wide smile.

"Like the most beautiful bride ever to present herself to a groom."

Violet blushed and smirked. "Get on with you, flatterer."

"It's not flattery. I speak the truth. Happiness is making you glow. And that is the loveliest shade of lavender I've ever seen you wear. I can guarantee your new husband isn't going to hear a word the priest has to say this morning."

Violet's colour remained high, but she seemed pleased by her niece's words.

"Can you believe Lester has come?" Violet asked, changing the subject.

Lillian kept her smile in place despite the drop in her mood. It was the one sore spot in the entire pot of happiness that was swirling around all of them. The viscount seemed truly chastened by the arrest of his steward and had come to wish his stepmother well on her new marriage. Lillian was glad for her aunt since the dear woman hated the thought of there being bad blood between her and her stepson. But the bounder had never seen fit to apologize to Lillian for the trouble he had put her through for an entire year. It was true that he was making at least a half-hearted effort to be pleasant or at least polite toward her, but Lillian couldn't truly be comfortable in his presence and was glad that he would be leaving after the wedding breakfast.

Brock was no more happy about having Lester there than she was. He had laughed with her about how to behave with the viscount, considering the pretence he had put on at the house party, but Lillian knew he was uncomfortable about his involvement in the investigation that resulted in the Ashburn Place steward's arrest.

Lillian and Brock had both been surprised the night before when Lester had quietly asked them for help in hiring a new steward.

"I suppose you've heard about the arrest," Shepley began without preamble.

"Very little, actually," Brock answered while Lillian kept her lips tightly sealed.

"Can't believe I was harbouring a traitor. And he tried to get me tied up in his mess. How could he have been in league with the French?"

"The French, you say?" Lillian admired Brock's ability to sound so surprised, despite the fact that she knew he was well aware of the facts.

"Can you imagine they wanted to kidnap Prinny? They were going to hold him for ransom. Something about some laws being passed. I didn't understand what the agents were telling me. Ralph was snivelling that they didn't mean him any harm, that they never would have hurt His Highness, but the agents said they likely would have killed him. And Ralph was skimming from my books to fund this venture."

Brock made a sympathetic murmur but couldn't reply.

"Nearly cast up my accounts when they told me about it. The agents said they would have arrested me over it, too, but they had some sort of proof that I was merely stupid, not guilty."

Lillian bit her lip and avoided Brock's gaze over that statement.

"I couldn't even argue with the man, could I? They never did tell me what their proof was. I didn't argue when they carted Ralph off. He was pleading for me to defend him, but I couldn't keep a traitor in the house no matter how my father might have trusted him. Clearly, my father was wrong about him after all."

"Your father was a fine man, Shepley. It's possible your steward changed his allegiances after the viscount's death."

Lester shrugged. "Anyhow, Ashburn Place is now free of Ralph, but I'll need to replace him quickly. I haven't the first idea how to go on though." He cleared his throat, looking uncomfortable, his eyes shifting between Brock and Lillian. "I need your help."

Lillian bit her lip. It was likely the closest he would come to acknowledging all that she had done to look after his estate since his father's death. A part of her wanted to leave him to fend for himself, but she had a strong sense of responsibility toward her late uncle and the estate she had so loved.

"Mr. Johnson's son knows about as much about the property as he does and would be happy for the promotion."

"The butler?" Lester sounded appalled at the thought.

Lillian fought against the sneer wanting to mar her face. "Yes, your butler has a grown son who would fill the position nicely, I would think."

Lester looked unconvinced but didn't argue the point.

Lillian blinked away the memory and returned her focus to her aunt. They were both going to get the happily ever after Violet had been wishing for. She was puzzled by the frown marring her aunt's forehead.

"What's wrong? Your glow is dimming."

This brought a grin back to Violet's face, but the older woman shook her head. "I'm afraid I'm going to wake up and find out it has all been a pleasant dream."

Lillian laughed. "You have strange ideas of what's pleasant, Aunt Vi. There have been enough unpleasant bits to reassure me that this is our reality. You are marrying a man who is thrilled to have you, and you're going to get to be a grandmother and be happy for the rest of your days."

Violet's grin returned. "And then it will be your turn soon. Can I be grandma to your babies, too?"

"Aunt Vi," Lillian protested with heat filling her cheeks. "I'm not even officially betrothed yet. Don't have me with child beforehand."

The two fond relatives shared a grin before Violet pronounced with satisfaction, "That's only a matter of time, my dear. Your earl has only awaited your betrothal out of respect for my wishes. Which says a great deal about what kind of man he is."

"Yes, it does," Lillian agreed as she watched the maid admit Brock, and he walked toward them. She could tell he was trying to not stare too obviously at her. This was to be Lady Violet's special day after all.

"You look wonderful, my lady," he said as he bowed over Violet's hand. "Might I have the honour of escorting you two to the chapel?"

"It would be our pleasure," Violet answered with a giggle.

Lillian and Brock exchanged a glance. Brock squeezed her hand as Violet stood from the stool she was still perched on, and then he offered them each one of his elbows.

Lillian felt her tummy dip with butterflies as she exchanged one more loving glance with the earl before fixing her gaze straight ahead. It would not do to fall into his arms during her aunt's wedding ceremony. That could keep a little while longer, she reminded herself with a smug smile as she tried to concentrate on the matters at hand. It wouldn't do to ignore her aunt's vows in favour of anticipating the glowing future Brock was offering her. He had been right. Being a countess was going to be far better than being a steward, she thought with a grin as she basked in the glow from her betrothed's loving gaze.

The End

About the Author

I've been writing pretty much since I learned to read when I was five years old. Of course, those early efforts were basically only something a mother could love :-). I put writing aside after I left school and stuck with reading. I am an avid reader. I love words. I will read anything, even the cereal box, signs, posters, etc. But my true love is novels.

Almost ten years ago my husband dared me to write a book instead of always reading them. I didn't think I'd be able to do it, but to my surprise I love writing. Those early efforts eventually became my first published book – *Tempting the Earl* (published by Avalon Books in 2010). There were some ups and downs in my publishing efforts. My first publisher was sold and I became an "orphan" author, back to the drawing board of trying to find a publishing house. It has been a thrilling adventure as I learned to navigate the world of publishing.

I believe firmly that everyone deserves a happily ever after. I want my readers to be able to escape from the everyday for a little while and feel upbeat and refreshed when they get to the end of my books.

When not reading or writing, I can be found traipsing around my neighborhood admiring the dogs and greenery or travelling the world with my favorite companion.

Stay in touch:

Website/sign up for my newsletter:
www.wendymayandrews.com
Facebook:
www.facebook.com/groups/WMASweetRomanceReadersAndFriends
Instagram:
www.instagram.com/WendyMayAndrews
Twitter:
www.twitter.com/WendyMayAndrews

Inheriting Trouble

The inheritance was meant to better her life, not muddle it.

Georgia Holton, wellborn but nearly penniless, is best friends with one of the Earl of Sherton's five daughters. When she is invited to accompany her friend for two weeks of the Season, Georgia jumps at the opportunity to have a little adventure away from her small village.

The Earl of Crossley is handsome, wealthy, widowed, and jaded. He has no intention of courting any of this Season's debutantes. After all, every woman he's ever known has been dishonest, including his late wife. But when a chance encounter throws him into contact with the Sherton ladies and their lovely friend, he can't help being drawn to Georgia's beauty and endearing personality.

When confusion about Georgia's small inheritance becomes known, a sense of obligation to right a wrong forces the earl and Georgia into close association.

But is she really different from any of the other women, or does she have an ulterior motive?

And can Georgia even consider getting close to a man from High Society, when all she wants is to return to her simple village life?

Sparks fly between these two, but it will take forgiveness and understanding on both their parts to reach a happily ever after.

Available now on Amazon

If you like Regencies with a touch of adventure, you will love the Mayfair Mayhem series. Book 1:

The Duke Conspiracy

Anything is possible with a spying debutante, a duke, and a conspiracy.

Growing up, Rose and Alex were the best of friends until their families became embroiled in a feud. Now, the Season is throwing them into each other's company. Despite the spark of attraction they might feel for one another, they each want very different things in life, besides needing to support their own family's side in the dispute.

Miss Rosamund Smythe is finding the Season to be a dead bore after spying with her father, a baron diplomat, in Vienna. She wants more out of life than just being some nobleman's wife. When she overhears a plot to entrap Alex into a marriage of convenience, her intrigue and some last vestige of loyalty causes them to overcome the feud.

His Grace, Alexander Milton, the Duke of Wrentham, wants a quiet life with a "proper" wife after his tumultuous childhood. His parents had fought viciously, lied often, and Alex had hated it all.

Rose's meddling puts her in danger. Alex will have to leave the simple peace he craves to claim a love he never could have imagined. Can they claim their happily ever after despite the turmoil?

Available now on <u>Amazon</u>

If you like Regencies with a touch of adventure, you will love the Mayfair Mayhem series. Book 1:

The Governess' Debut

The governess must charm both the spoiled child and the haughty earl.

Orphaned and destitute, gently born Felicia Scott must find a way to keep a roof over her head. No longer able to enter the Marriage Mart, but also not of the servant class, the only option is to find a position as governess.

After his spoiled, seven year old daughter has sent off three governesses in the 18 months since her mother died, the Earl of Standish doubts the young, inexperienced Miss Scott could possible manage the position. Since he's desperate and she comes so highly recommended, the earl agrees to give her a chance. Much to everyone's amazement, the beautiful, young governess succeeds where the others had failed. The entire household benefits from the calm, including the jaded earl.

How does he overcome his arrogance to see his governess' true value?

Available now on <u>Amazon</u>

Printed in Great Britain
by Amazon

65020459R00104